Tracing Iris

Other books by Genni Gunn

FICTION
Thrice Upon A Time
On The Road

POETRY
Mating in Captivity

TRANSLATION
Devour Me Too
Traveling in the Gait of a Fox

Tracing Iris

A NOVEL BY

Genni Gunn

RAINCOAST BOOKS

Vancouver

Raincoast Books acknowledges the ongoing support of the Canada Council; the British Columbia Ministry of Small Business, Tourism and Culture through the BC Arts Council; and the Government of Canada through the Book Publishing Industry Development Program (BPIDP).

First published in 2001 by
Raincoast Books
9050 Shaughnessy Street
Vancouver, B.C.
V6P 6E5
www.raincoast.com

Cover photo © Hulton Getty
Cover design by Val Speidel

1 2 3 4 5 6 7 8 9 10
National Library of Canada Cataloguing in Publication Data

Gunn, Genni, 1949-
   Tracing Iris
   ISBN 1-55192-486-2

I. Title.
PS8563.U572T72 2001   C813'.54   C2001-910845-1
PR9199.3.G792T72 2001

At Raincoast Books we are committed to protecting the environment and to the responsible use of natural resources. We are acting on this commitment by working with suppliers and printers to phase out our use of paper produced from ancient forests — this book is one step towards that goal. It is printed on 100% ancient-forest-free paper (100% post-consumer recycled), processed chlorine- and acid-free, and supplied by New Leaf Paper; it is printed with vegetable-based inks by Friesens. For further information, visit our website at www.raincoast.com. We are working with Markets Initiative (www.oldgrowthfree.com) on this project.

Printed and bound in Canada

For Frank

Contents

ANCIENT FOREST RISES IN SURF

March 12, 1998

NESKOWIN, Oregon. Like gnarled fingers rising from the surf, hundreds of stumps from an ancient forest buried at the time of Jesus are slowly being uncovered by El Niño's pounding waves.

It's a dumbfounding sight for people who have been making an almost religious pilgrimage to the rugged coastline to see the more than 200 stumps poking up from the beach ....

Brad Cain, ASSOCIATED PRESS

Extinctions

The first time she saw a dead body, Kate was crossing the bridge into Wenatchee. The man lay on the steep bank, face down, naked, his skin a startling white in the yellow dust. An ambulance was parked on the shoulder, and the attendants leaned against it, smoking. Kate could hear loud hard-rock music coming from the car radio of a couple who, like her, had slowed down for a look. She wondered who the man was and why he was naked. It seemed symbolic, somehow, as if he had just been reborn and would, at any moment, lift his head, put on his clothes and begin a new life. This made her think of Lethe, the mythological river of oblivion where, before rebirth, the dead drink to forget their former lives and sins. Had the dead man purposely thrown himself into the river? She was able to ponder this because the man was unknown to her and because Kate, too, was a stranger, a visitor passing through on her way to Pateros where her new husband waited.

She is reminded of the dead man now, two years later,

as she crosses a different bridge, the interface between her present and her past which, try as she might, she has not forgotten.

She is here in Twisp, Washington, that godforsaken, end-of-the-highway-in-winter town where her father still lives, because two days ago, his second wife, Elaine, fell into the river and drowned. *Finally gone.* What astounds Kate — who has waited so long for this moment, who spent years of her childhood fantasizing about it — is that she feels nothing. Or perhaps, a small twist of guilt, as if she were somehow responsible, simply by the act of longing.

Dead stepmother. In fairy tales, this is the part where the daughter rises, triumphant — freed from wicked spells and evil potions — to be joyously reunited with her father.

Of course, they live happily-ever-after.

"You must go home," her aunt, Rose, said when they heard the news. "Your dad has something important to tell you."

Home. From Vancouver, a six-hour drive, Kate's foot reluctant on the gas pedal. Direction: south on I-5, east at Burlington, continue on the North Cascades Highway for two hundred miles to Twisp. Bearing: Dad, childhood. Well, here she is.

Past the bridge, she stares upstream, as if she expects to see Elaine floating, belly-up, toward her. But the river yields only the tumble of water over stones, a sound that transports her to a Mexican beach, the melancholy strings of a guitar, the trickle of a water stick turned end to end, *Ray*. She hasn't seen her ex-husband for a year and a half. A familiar chill begins to spread in her chest, in her head, fills all the spaces. Suspended animation.

From the outside, however, she appears composed, having learned long ago to suppress the ice storm in her veins, or at least, the knowledge that it exists, in the way a skier must suppress the awareness that an avalanche could, at any moment, bury her.

If you could watch her drive into Twisp, you would see an attractive young woman in a crisp white shirt tucked into blue jeans, with brown city boots to match her camel blazer. Her shoulder-length black hair is secured into a ponytail by a tortoise-shell barrette. She wears no makeup except lipstick — Skin — carefully painted inside Nude lipliner. Three years ago, she let several of her earring holes grow over, so that now she sports only two studs in each ear. She could be the star in a commercial for toothpaste, or for the girl next door. You would hardly notice that when she reaches the police station where her father is Chief, her breath quickens.

Remember me, Dad?

Panic attack.

She coasts past two police cars parked in front, grips the steering wheel and forces herself to inhale slowly. Count to five. Hold. Count to five. Exhale slowly. Count to five. What she really wants to do is duck under the dashboard, like someone being shot at in a movie. Instead, she stares straight ahead and drives back to the highway. Eight more miles. She reminds herself that nobody gives a damn whether she's here or not. Her stomach is fluttery, unsettled. From her purse, she takes four antacid tablets and chews them slowly. The turmoil in her chest and abdomen begins to subside.

~

Had Kate's father, Joe, married someone else, Kate would have a mother.

She would probably still have grown up in Twisp along with the other children in her grade. She might have married Matt, her high-school sweetheart, or gone to university in Seattle or Spokane after graduation. She could have returned to Twisp, and be there now, with children of her own, attending townhall meetings, ardent in the fight against monster-homes and proposed condo developments, swearing to help protect the Methow Valley's fragile ecological balance. She might be wearing sensible shoes and tending a vegetable garden. During tourist season, she would probably work part-time in one of the shops or restaurants along the boardwalk in nearby Winthrop. Or she might turn her home into a bed and breakfast, serve homemade peach preserves on steaming muffins and tell strangers the familiar stories: the flood in 1948, before she was born, when the river rose to the deck railing; the Smokejumper's Base, with its helicopters and firefighting parachutists; how the valley once was filled with cattle ranches, orchards, sheep farms, homesteaders. She'd probably sigh, then grumble about the wealthy landowners coming in from The Coast, raising prices sky-high so the locals can't afford to own any more. She'd point to Sun Mountain and check the snow line, tell tourists they'd better head home soon, before the avalanches start up in the pass.

She would not have spent her teen years living with her aunt, Rose, in Vancouver, banished from her father's house, resentful of his new wife, Elaine. She might never have studied anthropology, or gone to work on the cruise ships, telling her brand of stories — of extinction and survival. She might not have spent so much time waiting to be abandoned over and over again.

~

To reach Kate's father's house, you take the Twisp-Carleton road south of Twisp for eight miles, then turn left onto a gravel road marked only by a green post, its paint flaked and blistered. Drive a quarter mile through an orchard of apple trees planted in haphazard rows — like a field of injured soldiers — extending down to the riverbank, and there it is, at the end. The house was built in the 1920s, and although Joe has modernized it several times — new kitchen, a bathroom beside the mud room, a wood-burning airtight stove in the living room — the rooms are small and dark, and the floor sounds hollow underfoot.

Kate climbs the stairs and sits on the top step until, slowly, the sky turns from indigo to onyx. Behind her, the covered porch stretches its weathered wood, nail-heads lifting like spring worms. It was here that her mother balanced on stilts, that her father explained how babies were made, here that she kissed a boy for the first time. Right now, however, Kate remembers only the last time she sat on this step, crying, while her father packed her suitcases into the car so he could take her to Vancouver to live with Rose. She was fifteen. Now, she's thirty-four and still brooding.

She sees the lights of his Explorer first, bouncing toward her, illuminating the fat red apples in the orchard on both sides of the driveway. Then, his silhouette inside. She imagines how she must look to him, caught in the glare. She doesn't rise, but waits for him to shut off the lights and cut the engine, waits for him to step out, slam the door and walk toward her, his navy windbreaker crackling with every step.

"So you've come." He stares at her, his eyes narrow, accusing. She has to stifle the urge to stick her fingers in her ears. His glare is hypnotic, tick-tocking her back, back, to sullen fifteen, fourteen, thirteen .... She holds her breath. "It's too late," he says, and climbs the stairs, brushes past her to the door.

Too late? She grows back into herself, scours her brain for words. *Gross stress,* she thinks, escaping to that place in her head where things are ordered. GROSS STRESS: A TERM USUALLY APPLIED TO COMBAT OR COMMUNITY DISASTERS SUCH AS CYCLONES, FLOODS, EARTHQUAKES ... *family reunions* ... AND TIDAL WAVES, ITS ANALYSIS ESSENTIAL TO THE UNDERSTANDING OF SURVIVAL-EXTINCTION SITUATIONS. She seeks refuge in the words *anticipatory, impact, recoil, post-traumatic,* aware of her own rising hysteria. It takes immense effort to say "Dad."

He stops without turning.

"I'm sorry about Elaine. I mean, not just about her now ... about everything ... about us ...." She flaps her hands in the air, as if to swat away all that's gone wrong between them.

He turns then and sighs. "You think you can change it all by saying you're sorry? Well, you can't, Kate. This isn't like playing hooky or dinging the car ... this isn't some stupid little prank. You can't fix it," he says.

And she sinks back to thirteen, joyriding her bicycle into his car, to fourteen, skinny-dipping at Ross Lake or prowling around Alder Mine on a Saturday night. And he's in his police car, worried, and tracking her down. She thinks of the calendar tacked to Rose's corkboard and imagines this year's caption: 1997: DAD REFUSES TO FORGIVE KATE.

She hugs her knees, shoulders slumped, head thrust forward and begins to rock. Her father can't see her, stiff and bursting as he is with his own memories.

Fix. A necessity. We can fix a car, a tire, a leak; we can fix a space station, a nuclear plant, an ailing heart.

She stops rocking, tense, breath held. Hears his swell in the silence.

He unlocks the door before he speaks. "Things have changed, Kate. You've been gone a long time."

"I can stay at a motel," she says, not sure what he means.

"I never put you out," he says.

His words drop like cold water into hot oil. She'd like to shout THAT'S EXACTLY WHAT YOU DID! Instead, she stares at the skeletons of trees, arthritic limbs warped and misshapen. *If anyone should beg forgiveness ....*

"You'd better come inside," he says, finally. "The funeral's tomorrow."

Once across the threshold, she is assailed by the unfamiliar. Gone are the veneer paneling and gold linoleum. In their place, ivory walls, ceramic tile and a synthetic area rug with a Chinese-cut flower border in pale greens and blues. Elaine, she thinks, certainly not Dad, her memories gliding along a familiar railtrack in her brain. She stares at the department-store couch and chair, the maple side tables, the giant TV screen and two card tables piled high with books, magazines, cups and glasses. *Derail.* What she does recognize are the dining-room set — oak table and eight chairs with cracked leather seats — and the La-Z-Boy with its footrest permanently stuck in the out position.

What did she expect? This is no fairy tale, and she is not awakening from an enchanted sleep.

The problem with fairy tales, she thinks, is that mothers often abandon daughters.

The problem with fairy tales, she thinks, is that fathers often banish daughters.

~

When she was small, Kate believed everyone who died went to live in a gigantic palace called The Everlasting Kingdom of Heaven. In church on Sundays, while the minister's voice droned, she imagined kings and queens and princesses in frothy pink dresses. She could never concentrate long enough to imagine "everlasting," but the word seemed fitting for Heaven, which was in the sky and invisible, anyway.

At first, she only visualized animals up there, because theirs was the only death she was familiar with. She didn't yet understand the concept of spirits and, when her cat died and her father said it went to Heaven, she imagined the cat, bum leg and all, preening itself up there with a trillion other animals. She wondered how, side by side, these predators and prey managed not to fight and kill each other.

When the old postmaster died, Kate added humans to Heaven. At his memorial service, she clutched her father's hand, afraid the casket might open and the postmaster might fly up, right there in front of her, "to answer God's call."

Later, her father explained that only *spirits* went to Heaven, that bodies remained here on earth. She couldn't understand where all those dead bodies went, until she dug up her cat's grave and found only bone fragments and discoloured fur — the cat's body both present but altered, like sugar immersed in water.

Her fascination with Heaven continued until her mother, Iris, abandoned Kate and her father. Kate had no idea where her mother was, or if she was coming back from Hell, where people said her mother had gone. Unable to visualize this new location, she decided her mother had flown to Heaven — even though she was not dead — and joined the crowds looking down from the stands, watching over the people on earth, watching over Kate.

Later, when Kate discovered ice ages, extinct species and cynicism, she banished her mother from Heaven and Heaven from her thoughts.

~

She hauls her suitcase up to her old room. Not that it looks like her old room; Elaine has turned it into a sewing/guest room. Only the bed is familiar, in the way something is in memory, although she doesn't recognize the frilly burgundy spread or the pillow shams.

A roar begins in her head, and she sinks into the mattress, fingers pressed into her temples to stifle the memories that threaten to land in a heap around her, artifacts to be examined, understood, reconstructed. The Everlasting Kingdom of Disasters.

From her purse, she takes a diazepam and swallows it. *Elaine.* She gets up and stares at the large cutting table pushed against one wall, piled high with a quilt-in-progress. In the middle, a stack of finished squares, like templates, the colours light on the outside, gaining in intensity as they near the centre where they converge into a black hole. Kate fingers this focused darkness, imagines Elaine spiraling in a tunnel toward some perceived light, perhaps, some everlasting happiness. All around the tabletop, dozens of tiny fabric squares, precut and stacked into tidy piles. A yellow Post-it note is stuck to the top of the largest square, with specific instructions as to how to proceed. She frowns. Did Elaine leave it there hoping someone would finish it? Or were the instructions for herself?

She goes to the window and stares at the gnarled trunks, drooping branches, ruddy apples. *Nothing's resolved.* She has spent the last nineteen years blaming Elaine for everything that has gone wrong, and now that Elaine is dead, she still has no idea how to trust someone, how to have more than a flimsy relationship, how to drink less, save more money, work reasonable hours, drive defensively, pay her rent on time and become a great judge of character. Self-pity wells in her eyes.

Kate is not usually this self-indulgent, but today she feels weepy and exposed, as if someone has shucked away her outer shell. *Stop it!* she tells herself. *You are a visitor here.*

She opens the closet: THREE SUMMER DRESSES, FOUR SHORT-SLEEVED SHIRTS, TWO PAIRS OF TWILL KHAKI PANTS, A RUSSET VELVET SKIRT UNDER PLASTIC AND TWO PAIRS OF SUMMER SANDALS IN THEIR ORIGINAL BOXES. SIZE 6½AA. *Middle-aged female, c.1990s.* Stop it, she tells herself as she continues to open and examine drawers: FOLDED COTTON HIGH-RISE PANTIES, 38 C BRAS, THREE PAIRS OF SUPPORT HOSE, FIVE CLAY SANDALWOOD BEADS. *Meticulous, sensory.* It's a reflex, this cataloguing mode. Kate is an industrial anthropologist, a consultant. SWEAT PANTS, WHITE SOCKS, TWO GREY T-SHIRTS under which is hidden THE JOY OF SEX. *Active, sexually curious.* Corporations hire her to study and explore the culture within their factories. One month she's working for a refrigeration company, trying to gauge workers' needs, the next she's investigating the relationship between immigrant meatpackers and their supervisors after a wildcat strike. Last month she recorded the folk knowledge of workers so that it could be incorporated into training programs. A GIDEON BIBLE — 1982 EDITION, A WHITE-ORCHID TISSUE BOX, AN OLD-FASHIONED KEY, C.1840S, COUGH DROPS. *Permanent bedroom, not guestroom.* Stop it, she tells herself again. These are not artifacts. She slides the bedside drawer shut, and begins to unpack.

She picks up her suitcase and opens it on the bed, but immediately she knows she can't hang her clothes next to Elaine's, any more than she could live next to her in this house. She slams the lid. It won't be the first time she's lived out of a suitcase.

Downstairs, her father has poured himself a drink and is sitting in the recliner, newspaper in hand, radio tuned to a soft-rock station. When she comes in, he stares at her intently.

"You look just like your mother," he says softly.

Kate frowns. What a strange thing to say, considering Iris was twenty-one the last time they saw her. Strange, too, that her father would speak of the distant rather than the recent past. But then, that's where their stories are fixed in time. A common narrative. One version.

"Seen her lately?" Kate asks in her casual voice.

"You're still waiting," he says and shakes his head.

She shrugs. "Got anything to drink around here?"

He looks hard at her. She stares back, defiant, challenging him. It's as if they're in a weather inversion, socked in by their cumulus past.

"There's tea and coffee in the kitchen," he says, finally, averting his eyes. "Or pour yourself a drink, if you'd rather." He nods toward the sideboard, at the half-full bottles of vodka, gin, scotch, rum. "Glasses in the cupboard over there. Mix in the fridge."

"Thanks." She busies herself pouring a scotch, then goes to the kitchen and knocks out a couple of ice cubes, wondering how much he knows about her drinking habits. When she returns to the living room, she begins to catalogue again. ICE-BLUE T-SHIRT, JEANS. *Looks years younger than fifty-nine.* BLACK HAIR, THICK, UNRULY. A STREAK OF GREY. FLAT BELLY, MUSCULAR ARMS. She supposes the orchard keeps him fit. When she was small, he used to let her help him. She couldn't have been more than six when she started carrying her tiny pail of apples — *careful, careful, you don't want to bruise them* — and climbing the ladder, to be exactly like Daddy. Did Elaine help him prune and spray and harvest? Did she climb down the bank, toward the cellar at the edge of the river — *careful, careful, you don't want to slip* — into the water's magnetism?

"What happened?" she asks, sinking into the couch.

He explains in bits and pieces, out of sequence. She listens. *To evaluate information, you must ask yourself: What is left out?* The day Elaine died, her father tells her, he went to work as usual, then on to an evening appointment. *Where?* When he returned, he assumed Elaine was asleep. *Separate bedrooms.* At dawn, he was awakened to the news that Elaine had been found floating a mile downriver. *Steady voice, dry eyes.*

"What I can't bear," he says, "is knowing that all those hours, all that time I was carrying on, she was in the water, cold and alone."

Omissions. "How did she fall?"

"She could have tripped, or had a heart attack or

stroke." He pauses. "The autopsy report should be in today," he says, as if this will explain it all, as if he expects that they'll slice open Elaine's chest cavity and pull out a small diary.

"I thought it was an accident," Kate says. "Why do they need an autopsy?"

He sighs. "She could have been killed, then dumped," he says, matter-of-fact. "They have to determine cause and time of death. For the record."

Killed and dumped. Kate imagines drug cartels and pornography rings, embezzlement, corporate frauds, mobsters.

"Who'd want to kill Elaine?" she says, and sips her scotch. When her father doesn't reply, her words widen and echo in the silence like a smoldering accusation.

"What do *you* know about us?" he snaps.

"As much as you know about me."

They glare at each other for a moment. She sets her drink down on the coffee table, crosses her arms and buries her hands in her armpits so he won't see them tremble.

"Let's not start something, Kate," he says, his voice subdued. He sets his paper down and goes to the window.

Nineteen years and he didn't even embrace me.

"Elaine loved it here," he says.

I loved it here too. Hot tears spring to her eyes and she looks away, angry at herself. "Rose said you had something to tell me."

She senses him stiffening, his back still to her. For a moment, he hesitates, then turns. "Yes." He walks out of the room and she follows him, impatient, but he says nothing. She follows him through the kitchen, front room and up three steps, before he turns and says, "Wait here. I'll be right back."

She pours herself a second scotch. While she's getting ice, he returns with three large manila envelopes. He sits at the table, fingering the envelopes in front of him. "Sit down, Kate," he says.

He lifts the flap of one envelope and takes out a legal-size document, small type, two pages long. Then he turns to her. "Elaine left a will," he begins, "and you're her beneficiary."

"Me?" she says, incredulous.

"There's a house and some property up in Canada. Elaine inherited half of it when her parents died." He pauses. "The other half belongs to your mother."

"Iris?" She frowns, trying to make the connection. "What has my mother got to do with Elaine?"

He bites his lip. "I'm sorry about this, Kate. But it was Elaine's wish .... We were so young ... it was so long ago ... I promised her ...."

"What?" she says, impatient now, her heartbeat erratic. "What is it?"

"Elaine was your mother's sister."

She leans back in the chair. Breathe. Breathe. "Elaine ...," she begins, but doesn't know what to say. She tries to process this as technical information, but it's like opening corrupted files: DNA replication ... a substance that carries hereditary information ... relatives, Dad ... from generation to generation ... Elaine and I related ... the opposite of love is indifference ... must be able to duplicate, and thereby create copies of itself ... Dad and Iris and Elaine ... double chains ... adaptive variations occur as a result of a fulfillment of needs ... *it's not how much you lose but who* ....

"It's a long story," her father says, his body suddenly agile. He pulls out the bottom envelope and passes it to her, unopened. "It's all in there. Elaine wrote it herself for you to have someday."

An envelope, she thinks, her mind seizing the tangible. How marvelous. Stuff in your past, seal it and BINGO! Vanished. Her father leans forward, expectant. She stares at the envelope, thinking, *Pandora's box*, thinking, *Who does he think he is?* thinking, *That's what he did with me, stuffed me into a car and sent me off.*

"How could you have kept this from me?" she says and leans forward. "I had a right to know."

Her father flinches, slides his elbows slowly back, off the table. He sighs. "Sometimes we make decisions we later regret ...."

"What else haven't you told me?" she asks, and as she waits for his answer, she sees he is no longer her childhood Dad — the superhero, I'm-OK-you're-OK, everything's-fine Dad. Etched into the sides of his nose and the corners of his eyes are journeys she knows nothing about. Have he and Elaine always known where Iris is? Have they been corresponding with her all along?

He shakes his head. "There's nothing else —"

Her hands clench and unclench. "Does Rose know?"

"Of course."

Her breaths come shallow, as if she were at high altitude. A patch of ice begins to form in her chest. "Does everyone know?"

"No one else. Just Elaine, Rose, me and now you."

"But why?" she says.

He points to the sealed manila envelope. "It's all in there."

She stares at the paper, but all she can think of is a documentary she saw recently about germ warfare. If you filled a lightbulb with a deadly virus, then smashed it in a subway in New York, you would infect millions of people ... pandemic. The envelope is modestly full, a slight curve, not even enough to pucker the lick-down flap. "I want to hear it from you."

He takes off his reading glasses and slowly rubs his eyes. "When you were very small," he says, "two and a half or so, your mother left us for a year." He pauses. Kate waits. "Rose took you to live with her in Vancouver. I was working ... I ...." He shakes his head. "I used to come up to see you a couple of times a month. That's when I met Elaine and she and I ... started, you know ...."

"You had an affair with her," Kate says. "You knew

her that long ago?" She sees him introducing Elaine to her when she was fifteen — *I've met someone* — as if she were a stranger.

"We were young .... When your mother came back, Elaine and I stopped seeing each other. And I swear, Kate," he says, scout's-honour fingers up, "we had no contact for many years."

Every contact leaves a trace, she thinks. Bruised heart. Aching body. Longing. Desire.

"Elaine got married and it was only after her divorce that she came looking for me. We thought it best to leave the past behind, begin new. There was no point in dredging it all up."

"No point?" she says. "What about me? Didn't I have a right to know she was my aunt? She could have told me things about my mother. Do you know where Iris is? Have you lied to me about her too?" She takes a deep breath, dizzy with information. *Calm down.*

"I swear, Kate, I don't know. Elaine had no contact with her. As for the family history, Elaine left you what she knew and remembered." He points to the envelope again.

She stares at it. *Omissions.* Back home, she has journals, diaries, daybooks, photo albums, cards, letters, e-mail, her life's progression documented. She began tracking herself when she first arrived in Vancouver. Runaway, reborn at fifteen. Rose's basement is full of boxes labelled KATE: PERSONAL. *Omissions.* The envelope in front of her is thin, a small water stain in one corner through which she sees a child's imagined past: fairy-queen mother, loving king father and herself as the everlasting princess.

"This is some family," she says, her voice hard and bitter. "My mother's off running around somewhere and her sister's been sleeping with my dad. Great." She stares up at the ceiling thinking, *hereditary information, generation to generation, copies of itself.*

"Kate."

She sits up straight, her heart an icy pit in her chest. "What about my half of the property?" she says. "I could use the money."

He opens the third envelope and pulls out more legal papers, his eyes avoiding hers. "Elaine rented it out for a while, but it fell into disrepair and was condemned a few years back. She kept up the taxes but that's about it." His voice is professional now, like a lawyer's. "Thing is, you need your mother's signature in order to sell it."

"So, it's a worthless piece of junk," she says.

"It's worth something."

"Where is it?" she asks.

"Northern B.C. Place called Kitimat, I think, or near there anyway. You could build a new house on it," he says, as if this really were an option.

"Right," she says. "I'll build a new house, with no money, in some godforsaken place and do what?"

He shuffles the papers back into the envelopes and pushes them, along with the sealed one, across the table in front of her. She takes all three and gets up. "Is that it?"

"Both Elaine and your mother grew up in that house," he says. "Elaine didn't want to sell it, but you could talk to a lawyer up in Canada. Maybe Iris' share could be kept in trust for her."

"Didn't Elaine even *try* to find her?" she asks, her voice edgy.

He shakes his head. "They were estranged. Elaine didn't know Iris had left us until years after the fact. By then, it was too late. She put some ads in local newspapers, but nothing ever came of them."

"That's it, then," she says. Her stomach hurts. Upstairs she has Rolaids, Tylenol 3, Prozac, diazepam, Ativan. She turns to go.

"Kate," he says, and she thinks he's going to say he's sorry. "We did what we thought was best at the time."

"Yeah. Well."

In her room — Elaine's room — Kate stares at the envelope, at the sealed flap, imagining her mother's life compressed to fit inside: 32 megs of memories on a two-inch strip. Slot it into the motherboard. Watch a video clip. She lies on the bed, the envelope against her heart, where it rises and falls with each breath. Ghosts rattle against the flap. She will not set them free in this house. She makes her mind a black screen to absorb her thoughts, regulates her breath until she feels strangely calm, disassociated from the news. Nothing's changed. Iris is still gone; Elaine is still dead; her father is still betraying her. What's the difference? If she'd known

Elaine was her aunt, she might only have hated her more.

She concentrates, instead, on the property and what she would do with the money if she could sell it. She'd buy herself a little house in the city. She'd have a white-oak office full of books and artifacts, two phone lines and a blues CD collection. She'd take in every alley cat and wouldn't let any man move in.

~

Imagine a team of anthropologists hundreds of years in the future, standing here in this eerie rising of stumps, the driveway, the road, no longer visible in the thick underbrush. Imagine the town of Twisp vanished. In its place, the valley expands U-shaped, like a lazy ginger cat. Gone are the riding stables, the A-frames, the barns. Gone are the bales of hay, the cattle, the green-tilled land. All is an alien landscape — like youth, with its treacherous twists and turns.

Down the middle of the valley, the Methow River meanders through overgrown orchards and plains, slowly, at first, then accelerating in its descent like a rolling avalanche. If the anthropologists were to follow it forty miles downriver, they would find Pateros, where Kate's ex-husband, Ray, works from May to October. And there, among the orchards, would be the scent of apples, the residue of their love.

Or, you could imagine this same valley transformed

with the cancerous growth of high-density condos, every square inch bricked, walled or concreted into submission. Even the river, perhaps, has been piped and rechannelled. Gone are the orchards, the woods, anything green and alive. Fortunately, the Cascades remain, rising above the valley, too rugged to tame. Every hundred years or so, a flood reminds the inhabitants that once a river flowed here.

Whatever the scenario, the future anthropologists squat inside this house. They have dug twenty feet and discovered the vestiges of Kate's family.

ANKLE BRACELET: *Gypsy*, one anthropologist writes in her journal. *Vagabond, wanderer, bohemian.* The ankle bracelet belongs to Iris, given to her by Joe, when he was still young and passionate. She wore it on the porch those long summer nights, bells jingling with the sound of leaving.

REVOLVER: *C.1990s*, the anthropologist writes, *of the type issued to police officers. Law-abiding, authoritarian.*

CRACKED PORCELAIN: *Female child, toy.* The pieces form the head of Kate's favourite doll, her straw body and rubber limbs long disintegrated.

HEART LOCKET: *Lover. Woman.* This one is Elaine's. Crack open the heart. Inside, packed clay where faces used to be.

And grief, too, is exhumed.

NOVEMBER 24TH, the day Iris disappeared, a day Kate has observed each year, sometimes perversely timing her own departures to it.

A LETTER written to Iris when Kate was ten, when she needed a precise reason for her mother's leaving.

There they are on the porch, Joe and Kate, sitting on two foam cushions on the top step, both of them in their ski jackets, mittens and hats. Kate is staring up at the night sky, astonished by the miracle of stars, bewildered by infinity. Her eyelashes and the inside of her nose are crisp, tingly with frost. From a corner of the kitchen window, where the curtain has snagged on a chair, a sliver of yellow light escapes onto the steps and beyond, so that the hoarfrost of the trees and the rough planks of the porch sparkle.

"I don't know exactly why she left ...," her father says, voice trailing into the dusky air.

Kate has been trying to remember the awful thing she did to displease Iris, the thing that made Iris plunk her outside on the porch, in snow. Kate never saw her again. "Maybe she didn't like me," she says. "Maybe I did something —"

Joe grasps her by the shoulders and looks into her eyes. "Your mother *loved* you," he says, slowly, as if speaking a foreign tongue. "It broke her heart to leave you behind."

Dear Mother, the letter begins, *I hate you.*

~

In the morning, the incessant ring of the telephone awakens her. Twenty-two rings. She sits up and peers out the window. Her father's car is gone. Ten more rings. She goes downstairs and picks up the receiver.

"Kate?" Rose's voice, breathless. "Kate? I know you're there. I'm sorry ...."

How could you not have told me about Elaine? I trusted you. A pain whittles her stomach. She hangs up. What was the point of an M.A. in anthropology, seven years at university studying human beings from a biological, social and humanistic perspective, when she can hardly understand those around her.

After she showers and dresses, Kate takes Elaine's sealed manila envelope and drives the eight miles back to Twisp, past the red *Wenatchee World* newspaper boxes, until she comes to Angie's Roadside Diner — a beat-up low-lying bungalow whose windows are brilliant with neon signs from fourteen different distilleries. It sits on several acres of wooded land that borders a ravine. All around, construction: large pipes stacked by the road, a partial trench, heavy machinery everywhere.

Imagine, for a moment, those future anthropologists sifting through shards of cups, saucers, plates: MAKEUP KIT, TWENTY-TWO PAIRS OF SHOES, IRON BEDSTEAD: *Party-girl*. It's Angie who has always been Kate's best friend, despite the two hundred miles between them, or maybe because of it. Distance, an illusion of intimacy. OUTER SKIN, perfectly preserved, like a rubber glove. *Tough. Survivor.* A PADLOCKED SAFE in the shape of a heart. What the anthropologists won't know is that by age forty, Angie has managed to fit in two husbands, two divorces and a son by neither husband; and that she is neither sentimental nor calloused by all this.

Despite the eight years between them, Kate and Angie are bonded into friends by the intimate knowledge of each other's pasts. Their history began in spring 1967 when Kate's mother, Iris, swung onto horses for riding lessons that stretched from mid-afternoon to late evening. Kate was four and Angie, who was twelve, needed the babysitting money so she could run away from home. Angie read Harlequin romances while Kate dressed her doll on the porch. Years later, when Angie was eighteen, and had a baby of her own, Kate reciprocated. Perhaps what bound them even then was the understanding that love is not infinite, that it exists between two anchors — beginning and end.

In those days, Angie was no pseudo-mother for Kate. She was stumbling through her own teenage years: a painful, illegal abortion in Spokane, her parents' savage divorce, another unwanted pregnancy. She hardly had time to figure herself out.

Today they are vastly different, opposites formed to make a whole: Kate has a post-graduate degree, Angie didn't finish high school; while Kate scoffs at *Vogue*, Angie saves up money to have her breasts and buttocks raised; Kate watches documentaries, Angie gossips about soap operas. What they do well together is drink in noisy bars, book last-minute holidays and choose all the wrong men.

Kate turns into the wide gravel lot and parks next to an idling truck. For a moment, she hears herself tell Angie about Elaine, the suspension at work, the divorce, the tranquilizers, the booze, the days when she can't get up, the nights when she can't sleep, the everlasting betrayals. It's like dredging a sewer line back to the birth canal, each memory a germ. Fill a lightbulb, smash it at a family reunion. Pasts make excellent warfare. She picks up the envelope of Elaine's herstory and shakes it. It does not explode. For a manic moment, she imagines herself addressing the congregation at Elaine's funeral: rip open the envelope and recite Elaine's words like a lawyer in a courtroom, reading out the accused's prepared statement.

The moment passes.

She folds the envelope in two and locks it in the glove box.

Of course, she won't tell Angie anything, because she is not the confessional type. You will never see her on an afternoon talk show, revealing the details of her sex life; you won't hear her voice on a phone-in program seeking advice; you will not find her in a hot tub at a women's retreat, sharing her past. She believes there is a reason why the heart is secured behind a ribcage, why the brain is encircled by the fort of the skull. No need to hand out ammunition.

"Kate," Angie says and grins as soon as Kate steps into the diner. "Welcome home." Angie's the kind of woman

men look at — a Liz Taylor, *Who's-Afraid-of-Angie?* character — with short curly hair hennaed into an unnatural
purple-red. For the past ten years or so, she and Kate have
been fleeing to Seattle, Portland, Vegas. A couple of times,
they flew to Puerto Vallarta for quick flings with smooth
strangers. But not since Kate married and divorced Ray.

Angie hips the swinging half-door, wearing a black
pantsuit which, Kate thinks, makes her look like someone
else. "I never thought I'd see the day," she says embracing
Kate. They were together last month in Seattle: rock
concert, drinking binge, hangover.

"I'm doing it for Rose," Kate says. "She's got a main
event in Montreal and couldn't get away." Her aunt is a
concert promoter. This part, at least, is true.

"Some people have all the luck," Angie says, and
laughs. At the sink she rinses out her coffee cup. "Give
me a minute to lock up and we'll go." They're heading
for The Barn in Winthrop, for Elaine's funeral. Joe is
already there, waiting. Angie ducks into one of the
booths and says, "Get the baby ready, Patti. Time to go."
She turns to Kate and rolls her eyes before disappearing
into her living quarters at the back.

Patti. Ray's daughter. Kate winces, a tangle of guilt in
her stomach. She steps forward to peer into the booth
where the seventeen-year-old is flipping through a
motorcycle magazine, licking her third finger at each
page, pale green polish like a bruise on the short, stubby
nail. Her newborn sleeps in a bassinet, next to the

jukebox mounted on the wall.

In this fairy tale, the motherless girl is Patti, whose mother died of cancer when she was eight. Her father raised her through elementary school, then banished her to live a pathetic, small life with Angie and her son, Trevor, who is not a prince, but is the father of Patti's baby.

During her brief marriage to Ray, Kate was not transformed into the perfect mother nor the wicked stepmother.

"Hey," Kate says.

The teenager looks up, kohl-ringed raccoon eyes. "What the hell do *you* care?" she says, as if this were the continuation of a conversation they've been having, as if it hasn't been a year and a half since they saw each other. She flips her waist-long hair behind her shoulder, licks her finger and riffles through the magazine. Rustle, crackle, rip.

In Pateros, the summer before last, Kate and Patti and Ray were a tentative family, a trial. In the fall, Kate would retreat to work in Vancouver, and Patti would return to board with Angie during the school year as she'd done since she was twelve, when Ray began to winter in Mexico to "realize his full potential as a muralist."

"Are you all right?" Kate asks, aware these are not the right words. *I'm sorry your father sent you away. I'm sorry he chose me. I'm sorry your mother died and your life hasn't turned out the way you planned.*

"As if you give two bits what happens to me," Patti says. She stares at Kate, eyes narrow and challenging.

"You're here for the damn funeral," she says, then adds, "not that you gave a damn about Elaine, either."

"You're right about Elaine," Kate says and slides into the booth next to Patti, who shies from her. The baby stirs; one tiny fist pushes into the soft skin of her neck. "She's beautiful." Kate lightly strokes the newborn's hands.

Patti reaches into the bassinet. "She's *mine*," she says fiercely. She picks up the baby and rocks her against her breasts. "Are you and Daddy ...?"

"I haven't seen Ray in over a year."

"Nobody has," Patti says, her voice wavering.

"What's happened?" Kate asks. "Is something wrong?"

"There's nothing bloody wrong with her," Angie says, coming back in. "Come on, Patti. We haven't got all day."

For a moment, Patti's tough act is gone. Kate pulls her into a half embrace. If Patti had a mother, she would be doing homework in a bright little room with posters on the wall and pink teddy bears against a frilly bedspread. She'd be listening to rap and talking on the phone with her girlfriends. She'd be not cleaning her room and sneaking out to the local necking pullout, Cat's Eye, with boys. She'd be out walking with her perfect mother who'd listen to all her problems and fix them.

Just as quickly, Patti's face masks over. She elbows Kate out of the booth.

Angie turns out the lights, so that only the neon continues to glow. "We're late, people," she says and reaches for the empty bassinet. "For God's sake, Patti, get a clean diaper on that baby." She sighs, a loud, impatient sound.

While Patti goes into the back, Angie motions Kate outside, out of earshot. "What do you do, huh?" she says. "You know that Trevor got laid off ... and with the new baby ...." She nods toward the diner. "I bought them a trailer and I try to help out. What the hell more does she want?"

Unconditional love, Kate thinks. In Mexico, that Christmas with Ray, a seagull flew back and forth along the beachfront, trailing a long fishing line from its mouth, like a magic trick. She could only imagine the barbed hook in its throat, the parade of its inevitable death. It's the things you can't see that are barbed, she thinks: love, yearning, regret.

She sits on a hard auditorium chair in the front row, beside her father, trying not to stare at the open coffin, at Elaine's otherworldly greenish-grey skin. Instead, she imagines Elaine swimming in Acheron, the river of woe.

They're in the only place large enough to accommodate everyone for Elaine's memorial service. Joe has been Police Chief for thirty years: everyone knows him and loves him. In public, her father has always acted the extrovert. Humorous and courteous, he charms both men and women with his charades. When she lived here and people came to visit, Kate prayed they'd never leave.

"The Lord is my shepherd ...," the minister begins.

35

She listens to the fire-and-brimstone delivery, wondering why fear has to play such a large role in salvation, whether religion is simply afterlife insurance. Was Elaine religious? Or was she like a member of the Order of the Solar Temple, whose deaths were hedonistic and frivolous, instant tickets to Nirvana? Of course, this minister is not suggesting suicide. In fact, he has selected information from the autopsy report and rearranged it more comfortably, so that Elaine's death sounds benign.

"Brave ... courageous ... a full life," he says.

What the autopsy report confirmed is that Elaine drowned, after falling from a height against rocks, that she'd had a heart attack and that she was bruised and cut when they found her wedged between a tree branch and the shore. Kate would like to ask her father what had been wedged between them and when.

To evaluate information, you must ask yourself: what is left out?

What he left out is, *I miss her. I loved her.*

Kate stands and sits, according to convention, flanked by her father and Angie. She feels foreign, disconnected from the tremulous voices, the red-brimmed eyes, the outpouring of emotions. Her father's back is straight, his eyes clear, his handshake firm. Kate nods to people she hardly remembers, thinking, *To sustain a family image, the truth must be expended.* She is black fleece. Prodigal daughter. The spiteful offspring who never visits her father, a carbon-copy Iris. She concentrates on the candle-flickers on the wall, black shapes writhing in and around each other, distorted spectres.

It's only when the minister closes the lid of the casket that Kate feels a stirring in her chest. In that satin-flocked box with Elaine lie the past nineteen years. All Kate's yearning is futile, her imagined revised past a hologram in the air. Everything she has ever lost comes swimming to the surface — mother, father, lovers, husband, friends, jobs — an outpouring she can't control. She is fifteen, on the porch, begging her father to let her stay; she is twenty-two, alone at Christmas, while her married lover skis with his family; she is four years old, mother gone; she is then, now, sinking into a gaping pit of black sticky sorrow. The internal pressures of her past smash together like tectonic plates.

Beside her, her father shifts his weight from foot to foot.

Angie hands her a tissue and pats her back.

All year, an accumulation of loss. Pills, booze, nothing contains it. Loss should be weightless, Kate thinks, not heavy enough to crush her.

What she hasn't told anyone is that in January of this year she was appointed Lecturer in the Department of Anthropology at Starpike College. By early March, she'd been suspended and her contract was/is under review.

Her sins: she was a character reference for a colleague who had been charged with sexual harassment by one of his students. In his version, the female student went to his office and suggested they discuss her failing grade over dinner. He suggested she drop the course. The young woman left, but persisted in phone calls and e-mail, some of which were sexually explicit — communications the professor ignored. A month later, the young woman charged him.

While Kate found the story bizarre, she believed in the professor's innocence. Other colleagues also spoke on his behalf and after an inquiry, the young woman's charges were dismissed. Nothing more should have come of it except that, incensed, the student scrutinized all his supporters and discovered he and Kate were lovers, which in the context of the inquiry, was inappropriate behaviour. The case had been raging on chat lines, and the college was not too happy with Kate's name front and centre.

Sin #2 contributing to her suspension was her use of class time to "enlighten your students with your personal opinions," as the dean phrased it. What Kate had told her class was that she believed that this society found it difficult to acknowledge that women could be anything but goodness personified, and that women were capable of devious behaviour. She told them that forcing women up onto pedestals was as dangerous and oppressive as forcing them down into servitude and silence.

A fury of female students signed a complaint, and when this dispute ended up on the dean's desk, Kate received her carefully worded suspension (until a grudge of lawyers could comb through the files and make her dismissal legal).

She went home, bewildered, and examined the sequence of events. Although each event, in itself, was inconsequential, stacked together they seemed to reflect an intangible evil, abstract and undefined.

She went to a bar, drank till closing, then got into her car. She doesn't remember much about the drive or the crash. She doesn't remember much about that night.

When she came home from the hospital — her foot broken, a few cuts and bruises — she found in her mail slot her divorce papers from Ray. She sat on her couch and took stock: she'd lost her job, her driver's licence for three months, her ability to walk and her husband.

Back at the house, Angie installs herself in the kitchen, unwrapping tray after tray of luncheon foods. She has arranged the burial, the flowers, the psalms, the guest list and the food. "Your father was not in a position to do it," she explains. "Besides, it's no trouble."

Kate watches people's lips move, as if she were behind a pane of glass. She has washed her face and reapplied makeup.

Then Angie's at her side. "You OK?" she says and slides her arm around Kate's waist.

Kate shrugs.

Angie hands her a coffee. "Spiked," she whispers.

"Is it that obvious?" Kate says, taking it, grateful.

Angie touches her elbow, nods toward Joe, who is speaking with a young man. "You remember Matt."

It takes Kate a moment to register that Angie's talking about Kate's childhood sweetheart. Taller, more confident, but unmistakably Matt. He works with her father.

Matt turns and for a second, Kate feels herself propelled back to 1978, a year permanently burned into her brain as a year of disasters, of catastrophic events for which no one was prepared: the year her father married Elaine without telling her; the year the supertanker, the *Amoco Cadiz*, ran aground in the Brittany peninsula, releasing a widening, hook-shaped inkblot across the water — *Elaine, a menacing spill*; the year chemical waste buried for thirty-five years in Love Canal bubbled to the surface in backyards and basements; the year she and Matt were two teenagers racing toward Coeur d'Alene in his father's borrowed car, racing toward happily-ever-after.

Her father stopped them easily — a couple of phone calls, a road block — then sent Kate to Vancouver, brimming with first-love promises, sure Matt would follow on the proverbial white horse, over two hundred miles of broken glass. She swore she'd kill herself if he didn't come for her. And now, two decades have passed and he never kept his promise and, of course, she never killed herself.

The moment passes.

He smiles, raises his hand and comes toward her. Angie moves on.

I'd rather he stayed a perfect memory.

He holds out his hand. "Hello, Kate," he says, his voice intimate.

She smiles. "Matt." She thinks of all the things she saved up to say to him. For months in Vancouver, she waited, a suitcase under the bed. When her adult life was in shambles, she would conjure him up in soft focus, like the hero in a black-and-white movie. How perfect he became through the lens of distance and time. She looks up at him now. TALL, SLENDER. BLACK WAVY HAIR, BLEACHED-GREEN WHIRLPOOL EYES. She bites her lip and sips her coffee. *I have no idea who he's become.*

"You look wonderful," he says, smiling.

She recognizes the unspoken. "How have you been?" she asks.

He stares at her until she looks away. "Waiting to see you," he says.

She looks around and signals Angie.

"Excuse us for a moment, will you, Matt?" Angie touches Kate's elbow and leads her away. "Everything OK?" she whispers.

"Yeah. Thanks." Kate squeezes her hand. "You go on. I'm fine."

Angie winks, weaves back into the crowd. Kate stands to one side and watches her father receive people like the host at a party. In his stoic face and coiled body is her childhood dad, the one whose response to confrontation was a silent and retreating back. A maelstrom rises in her chest. *The opposite of love is indifference.* She looks into the room, and for a moment, all she sees are people's backs, their turning away. She presses her fingers into her temples and goes toward the stairs.

But Patti intercepts her on the bottom step. "I gotta talk to you," she says.

Kate tries to motion her to one side, but Patti persists. "Listen," she says. "I've got to get away from here ....." She lowers her voice. "From Trevor ... but all I got is my motorcycle and I can't take the baby on that. "

"Have you called your dad?" Kate's heart constricts, as if a safety valve were closing to guard against overflow.

"My *dad.*" Patti spits out the word. "He couldn't even fucking be bothered to come see the baby."

"He's not in Pateros?" Kate says, trying to keep the disappointment out of her voice.

Patti shakes her head. "Haven't seen him since summer before last." She pauses. "When you were there."

"He must be very busy," Kate says, aware of how false it sounds.

"We wouldn't be any trouble." Patti shakes her head. "You could take us with you when you go. Drop us off in Seattle."

Kate stalls. "I've got things to take care of first," she says, "and I don't know how long I'll be."

Patti stares at her, unblinking.

"Look," Kate says. "Call your dad and make some plans. Then, when I go, I promise that if nothing's resolved, we'll figure something out."

~

The day after Iris left, Joe took Kate to the Grand Coulee Dam. Then they drove down to Moses Lake for lunch and, on the way back, they found a stray kitten wobbling at the side of the highway. They took it home, and Kate named it NuNu and loved it excessively until it died of kidney failure when Kate was thirteen.

Actually, Kate does not remember Grand Coulee Dam or Moses Lake or even the cat on the highway, because she was only four at the time. Her father has recounted this story so often, it has *become* one of her memories. She is also familiar with that particular stretch of highway, so it is not difficult to superimpose a tour, a hamburger and fries, a small frightened kitten at the edge of a cliff. She envisions them all in pure summer, the sky an impossible sapphire, although she knows her mother left in late autumn — November 24, 1967.

What reminds her of all this is the calico cat sleeping on her bed. She didn't notice it yesterday and is surprised not by the cat but by the notion that her father cares for it. A sudden lump expands in her throat. She imagines her father alone, as he opens the can of cat food, bends down to fill the water bowl, strokes the soft fur. Kate pets the cat herself and it's like turning a switch — *Here I am*, the purr says. *Well, here I am, too*, Kate thinks.

43

She collects her jacket and purse and slips downstairs. The house is still crammed with people; her father still the extraordinary host. She walks past a cluster of subdued laughter, out into the cool darkness.

On the way to Winthrop, she thinks about Patti. *What do I know about mothering?* Kate shies away from emotionally needy men, women, situations. She doesn't join clubs, support groups or denominational anything; avoids Tupperware parties, singles' nights at local bars; ignores the Personals, Dear Abby and Ann Landers. When she does volunteer her time and expertise, it's to public causes — save the whales, stop logging Clayoquot, preserve a Native burial site — causes that allow her to retain personal distance.

Rose — who's a bit of a pop psychologist — calls Kate "hyper-vigilant," which Kate considers a positive rather than a negative. Rose has read many books on the subject, books she wishes Kate would read. Kate thinks it's all a bit of a crock. People should be more vigilant with their hearts and emotions; they should not spew them out at every opportunity.

Every now and then, when Kate needs to spew, she writes letters to Iris, letters which she no longer mails. What started out as a real correspondence when she was a child has became a box of dead mail. Kate thinks of her as *Iris* rather than *Mother*, because her memories are second-hand: photos she's seen, stories she's heard. The two of them as mother/daughter are an illusion.

Right now for example, if Iris were here, Kate imagines the two of them would duck into The Palace for a scotch, straight up. Maybe several. They could flirt with a couple of amusing men, check into a motel later. Iris, forever young.

Although it's early September, tourists swarm about — retirees on their way south, cyclists in fleece jackets here for the weekend races, young couples on honeymoons, gaggles of teenagers searching for each other. Kate chose Winthrop, even though there are bars in Twisp, of course — Mick & Miki's, Antler's, The Branding Iron, all on the main street. But if she's going to have a drink or two, she'd rather do it among strangers.

On both sides of the street, squares and rectangles of light from open shops fall across the boardwalks like discarded windowpanes. Winthrop is one of those towns that looks familiar even to those who come here for the first time. Mostly, this is because it has been restored to the universal ideal of a Western centennial town, with wooden buildings, quaint, squared storefronts, swinging saloon doors, hitching posts. Naturally, the wood is creosote-treated, the paint guaranteed for twenty years, the boardwalks solid and clean, the restrooms bright and sanitary with their HAVE YOU WASHED YOUR HANDS? signs above the sink. It all looks old, in the way old would look today, modern-technology old. And behind these facades, shopkeepers do a brisk business selling trendy T-shirts, cowboy hats, mountain bikes and hiking boots.

A tape loop of cars spins up and down the main street. Jeeps park in front of taverns, windows down, music thumping.

Kate follows the procession to The Palace, relieved to see bright clothes and smiles, to hear laughter and chatter. Here, nobody knows about Elaine. She wonders how many Elaines die each day everywhere, something happening all around while people watch, unmoved.

The tavern is three-quarters full, most people in their thirties. She chooses a stool at the tall bar in front of the dance floor and, even though her back is close to the wall, she feels conspicuous because her shirt and the seams of her jeans glow in black light. On stage, a blues trio is setting up. She orders a drink and watches them. The musicians are battle-scarred from too many drunken nights in too many towns. Middle-aged, they still wear tight jeans and have long hair, though their bellies flop over their belts and their hairlines are receding. She feels uncomfortable for them, wonders if they have families and pets, if they go to church Sundays and belong to the PTA, if they're locals and if they know her dad. She gulps a mouthful of scotch.

Then Matt's beside her. "Can I join you?"

She looks up, surprised. "Did you follow me?"

He shrugs, squeezes in beside her, his arm brushing hers. "I saw you leave. I wanted to speak to you."

She stares at her drink.

The band, now set up, begins a sound check. It's

impossible to speak above the screech of microphones, above the TESTING, TESTING, TESTING in various tones and decibels, *t*'s popping until properly equalized. For a moment, she's back in her transient life, and this is merely another bar she'll be out of soon.

"I know it's irrelevant now," Matt says, so close into her ear she can feel his breath, "but I've always wondered why you never answered my letters."

"What letters?"

"Didn't your father forward them?"

"I didn't get any letters."

"He wouldn't give me your address. He said he'd send them on."

"I can't believe Dad would have ...." As soon as she says it, though, she knows he did. "You could have asked Angie where I was," she says.

"I thought you were getting my letters. I had my pride too, you know." He smiles. "I was crazy about you."

A flush creeps up her cheek. "Anyway," she says, embarrassed, "we were children."

He signals the waitress for another round. They both watch the band members move cords, speakers and stands.

"Angie says you travel a lot. You always wanted to do that."

She sips her scotch. "And you," she says. "What happened? I didn't figure you for a police officer."

He shrugs, touches her shoulder lightly. "You can't always get what you want."

"The Stones."

The band concludes the sound check and shuts off the stage overheads. Only the coloured spots remain, softening the hard edges of the room.

"Are you married?" he asks, though she's sure he must know.

"I was. For a short while." How to explain that? She pauses. "You?"

"Twelve years. I've got an eight and a five-year-old." He seems relieved to have told her this.

She feels a small shift in balance. "Anyone I know?"

"From the coast. I met her in a commune down the road."

Kate smiles. "A commune? Nowadays?"

"There are seventy-two of them along the highway. Alternative lifestyle."

She wonders what this means. Is he talking about farming and living off the land? Or is he talking multiple sexual partners? "How alternative?" she says.

He explains that a group of young people from Seattle pooled money and bought a large parcel of land to farm organically. They built several cabins, worked the existing orchard and planted other crops, which they sold at the farmers' market. He talks in neutral tones, explaining the difficulties of irrigation, planting and harvesting seasons, as if he were speaking about the life of a stranger and not his wife.

"But she's not still doing it, surely?" Kate says, trying to nudge him into the present.

"Barbara's a schoolteacher now." He looks away, as if searching for words. "I'm always amazed at how things change," he says, softly. "One day you wake up in the middle of your life and you don't know how you got there."

She is startled by this admission. She blinks several times. What she can't tell him is that she was pregnant when she went to live with Rose, that she had an abortion. When he didn't contact her, she let Rose convince her. Their son would be eighteen now, had he lived. What she can't tell him is that for years she has dammed this out of her mind. That she feels disconnected, aborted herself. She used to read newspaper ads in which birth mothers and children searched for each other, pretending that her mother might try to find her this way, even though both her father and Rose still live in the same houses and are only a phone call away. What she can't tell him is that she, too, is bewildered to find herself here, now, alone.

She waits for the dangerous moment to pass, lifts her glass and drinks. "Yeah. Well. It's a life."

He looks at her, questioning. The band goes up to the stage and someone turns out all the lights, so that the air is tinted by neon beer signs and the crimson jars of candles on tables.

"Are you OK?" he asks.

She nods. "It's been difficult ...."

"I'm sorry about Elaine," he says, misunderstanding.

She sighs. "I hardly knew her. What was she like?"

"She was all right. In the end, I felt sorry for her, of course. It's a small town, and people talk." He moves his glass in a circular motion, clinking ice cubes.

She stares at her own glass. "What kind of talk?" she says, keeping her voice even.

"I'm sure there wasn't a kernel of truth in it. Angie and Joe have been good friends for years. "

She runs a hand through her hair, heart pounding.

"It's going to be really hard on your dad, all this. I'm glad you came home."

Home. She listens to the word in her head, to the tug of invisible strings.

Home on the range, home run, home free, homeward bound, homegrown, hometown, homebody. Alien sounds looping in her brain. *Home truth, homesick, homeless.*

"My coming here has nothing to do with him," Kate says and suddenly she knows. "I'm looking for my mother."

Adaptations

The past two summers, between consulting jobs, Kate has been hired as a lecturer on cruise ships. It's an easy gig: a ninety-minute talk each evening which, in layman's terms, explains a little more of our culture, the way we live and why. Her particular specialty is extinction and adaptation.

Some years ago, she and Angie took a road trip to Colorado and stopped at Mesa Verde, to look at the cliff dwellings of the <u>Anasazi</u>, a people who had inhabited the Four Corners Country — Southern Utah, Southwestern Colorado, northwestern New Mexico and northern Arizona from 200 to 1300 A.D. Kate was fascinated by the fact that in the space of one hundred years, the Anasazi had vanished. It seemed unlikely that they would all get up one day, gather their belongings and descend the steep, eight-thousand-foot mesa. Did they wander off, rename themselves and start new lives? Kate looked at the museum exhibits of their art and gathered brochures filled with puzzling explanations for their mysterious disappearance.

Back home, the Anasazi haunted her. She began to research other cases of tribal extinction. It had been years since she graduated from university and much of her knowledge had faded into a vague recollection of theories and discoveries, of peoples who were labelled and chronicled like lab animals, their cultures arrested in some distant past when an anthropologist spent three months in this or that remote location studying them. Kate, herself, back then was a naive scholarship student in love with her married professor. Had someone labelled and chronicled her, she'd be forever a stereotype in a TV movie, the injured other woman, perhaps.

Her fascination grew and the more she read about extinct species, the more she understood that nothing is static, least of all human social systems, and too often, anthropologists discuss their subjects as if they were objects fixed in time, freeze-frames, unresponsive to the dynamics of nature.

Change and adaptation are why we're here. So, why then, she wondered, do species become extinct? Is it their inability or unwillingness to change? Or are they victims of some catastrophic event? Does nature simply tire of some species and stop nurturing them, like mothers who abandon children? What began for Kate as an interest in extinction has grown into a passion even Rose, who is an obsessive personality, thinks is excessive.

For the cruise gig, Kate has amassed a series of stories about cultures on the verge of extinction, which she tells mostly to retirees hungry for diversion, urgent in their search for meaning.

July 24, 1997 / *Legend of the Seas*

THE KAIADILT

"Imagine, say, that all of you in this room are a tribe that's been living on an island so remote that you've had no contact with other cultures. You live off the land, eating wild berries and roots as your ancestors did before you. You haven't progressed to fishing and boat-building because the ocean around you is too dangerous to navigate. Perhaps years or centuries ago, someone tried it and capsized. You don't know that beyond your island, people jet the skies and cruise oceans, like we're doing now.

"Now imagine that slowly, possibly due to ozone depletion, air temperatures begin to rise — we've had a hotter summer than usual this year, haven't we? Your water sources dwindle. Your crops wither and food is hard to find. You haven't yet discovered how to make sunscreen so some of you are developing skin cancer.

This happens over several years so that you slowly adapt to the worsening conditions.

"What do you think you'd do? You can't get off the island and by now you're suffering from chronic health problems — starvation, dysentery, dehydration, you name it.

"The year is 1948. While elsewhere in the world, Israel was created, the Alaska Highway opened to civilian traffic, and the *Kinsey Report on Sexuality in the Human Male* was published, the Kaiadilt were still one of the world's most excluded and isolated cultures, probably the last group of coastal Aborigines to come in regular contact with white men. They lived on Bentinck Island, off the coast of Australia. As I described, for years they had suffered droughts, high air temperatures, poor water supply and solar radiation. Their physical and mental stress is so great that the people began to kill each other systematically. A man would be murdered, his wife appropriated and his children eaten. You can appreciate that a society that eats its young doesn't have much of a future.

"The Kaiadilt were surely heading for extinction when catastrophe struck: a tidal wave washed over Bentinck Island and salinated all their water holes. Without fresh water, their survival became so precarious that the remaining forty-seven inhabitants were evacuated to nearby Mornington Island.

"In the aftermath, the Kaiadilt interpreted the cause of their problems in interpersonal terms: it was a case of warfare and revenge. They had been concerned about sexual satisfaction — the need for women — rather than economic security, social status or children. Anthropologists defined their crisis as ecological stress caused by food and water shortages. An absence of life-support."

Mother goddess, mother figure, motherfucker, mother love, mother earth, motherlode, mother tongue, motherhood, motherless.

Kate thinks about the Kaiadilt in the car, driving north toward the border, north nine-hundred miles past the Canadian border to Iris' house in Kitimat. *My mother's house.* Her head feels light, as if she hasn't eaten for days or has been hiking at high altitude. *Deprivation*, she keeps thinking. *Life-support. Absence.* Nothing and everything has changed. *Dear Iris,* she begins, composing an imaginary letter in her head. *Dear Mother. When I was small, I used to pretend you would return at any moment. Sometimes, I'd dress up, just in case, because I wanted you to see me at my best.*

After Iris left, Kate wrote to her once a week — *Dear Mommy, I am fine.* — while she sat at the kitchen table, carefully drawing each letter of each word. Her father began teaching her the alphabet when she was two, so that by age four she could read and write letters to her mother.

Iris replied with postcards or brief notes, and once, on Kate's birthday, sent her a stuffed Donald Duck whose yellow rubber beak Kate sucked on for years when no one was looking. Then one day a few weeks before Kate started Grade 1, Iris wrote to say she was moving and would send her new address as soon as she was settled. Kate never heard from her again, but she continued to write Iris letters, not weekly, of course, but as the need arose — *Dear Perfect Ghost Mother* – letters she never sent and which, now, she can compose without writing.

Even as a child, Kate knew the real mothering was being done by her father, but this did not diminish her fascination with Iris. She wonders if Iris thinks of her as a ghost, if Kate is her perfect daughter.

What Kate has never understood is how Iris — any mother — could so easily substitute a lover for her child. Men come and go, and are often highly inappropriate. Kate is familiar with this variety: men with whom she has nothing in common; married men like Stephen, tied to wives and families; men like Ray, who live vast distances from her; and various Peter Pan men who can't be taken seriously. Kate often wonders if Iris stayed with the man she ran off with. Does Iris have other children? Are there half-brothers and half-sisters Kate might inadvertently meet and not recognize? She has a friend who, at his father's funeral, discovered his father had another wife and family. She found this extraordinary. How did he keep them apart in his heart? Did he relegate each family to a separate chamber? Didn't he worry they'd meet one day, on the tip of his tongue, when he accidentally named one for the other? What does Iris tell her other family?

Kate has imagined Iris kidnapped and held hostage for three decades. She has imagined Iris the amnesiac, searching for herself, door-to-door, across the planet. She has imagined a thousand improbable explanations. What she cannot imagine is that Iris doesn't care, and this, I suppose, makes her as myopic as the Kaiadilt, or perhaps, as adaptive. *Mother wit, mother's ruin.*

Patti. Before she left town, Kate knocked at the trailer, and when no one answered, she scribbled a quick note — *Patti, I had to leave unexpectedly. Will call you when I get back. Kate.* — and slid it under the door. Patti is Ray's responsibility; Patti is not her daughter. It's night, the time when guilt magnifies in direct proportion to darkness.

It's a good thing, then, that she can't hear the argument between Patti and Trevor hundreds of miles away, an argument that Angie, who is in the diner, can hear all too well — not the words they're using, but the tones: the familiar high-pitched hysteria of Patti's voice and the harsh gravel of Trevor's. She turns up the volume on the CD player, uncomfortable with the customers' furtive glances, with their downcast eyes. Finally, just past eleven, after the last customer has left, Angie turns over the sign to read CLOSED, and goes to the trailer. In the bedroom, Patti is furiously hurling clothing into a large suitcase and, as each item lands, Trevor pulls it out and throws it onto the floor. Jeans, jeans. Bra, bra. Panties, panties. Shirt, shirt. An assembly line, each fling a little harder, a little faster. Socks, socks. Shoes, shoes.

"What's going on?" Angie says, and they both turn to look at her.

Patti's eyelids are red and puffy, her eyes narrow and hostile. "None of your fucking business!" she shouts, and throws a T-shirt at Angie.

"You watch your tongue," Trevor says, then glares at Angie. "This is private. You can't just come in here whenever you want."

Angie's blood is hot and pulsing through the bluish vein across her temple. "*Private?*" she says. "This is *private*? The whole damn town's had to listen to you!" She points to both of them. "Either this stops, or you move out of here. And I mean it this time." She slams the trailer door, gets in her car and drives off.

It's a good thing all Kate can hear is a different Patti, one finely in tune: Patti LaBelle wailing in her four-octave range: "Somewhere over the rainbow / way up high ...." *Right*, Kate thinks. *Dream on.* She wonders what land she'll find in Kitimat.

Everyone's dead, she thinks. Grandma and Grandpa Mason, Oma and Grandpa Hinton and now Elaine. Only four left: Rose, Joe, Iris, Kate. End of the line. Kate never met Iris' parents — Oma and Grandpa Hinton —

who, her father said, refused to acknowledge both their daughter and granddaughter. When they died, years ago, Kate felt only resentment. She wonders now if this was another of her father's lies, if he orchestrated their hatred and indifference for his own ends. She finds it extraordinary that he could have been and continues to be so selfish so casually. Everything is shifting, she thinks, unstable, like plate tectonics, the side of a volcano, the ocean floor, the Berlin Wall.

Across the border, in Canada, she feels free. She told her father where she was going, and for once, appreciated his reserved silences, because she was afraid of what she might say once she started. All the things she didn't say have turned into air bubbles in her blood stream. She chews antacids and swallows diazepam.

Beside her on the seat, Elaine's manila envelope remains sealed. She'll open it at the house. Her home. Homecoming. A ritual return.

When she's standing inside the tumbledown two-storey outside of Kitimat, she doesn't feel anything close to return. Curiosity, yes. The house is sparsely furnished in accidental decor, as if through the years, tenants have whimsically removed and abandoned pieces. She has no way of knowing whether any of these belonged to her grandparents. There have been kids here recently — within the past couple of months — evidenced by beer cans, broken bottles, chocolate-bar wrappers and potato-chip bags flung into the fireplace, their surfaces too shiny to have gathered much dust.

The couch is torn; springs and thick matting spill out, discoloured with rust. Many windows are broken; some have jagged edges that form abstract icy landscapes against the forest green. In the crack of one of the sills, a weed has rooted.

She goes upstairs and explores the two bedrooms. On the floor of the largest is a double-size mattress, semen- and water-stained. Beer cans and bottles on the windowsill and, beside the mattress, a melamine plate with a candle melted to its middle. It reminds her of the secluded cabin in the mountains where she and Matt used to go when she was fourteen. It belonged to a Bellingham family who used it only in June and July. Matt forced a window open, climbed in and unlocked the door. They often escaped to the cabin on Saturdays through fall and winter, sometimes on his snowmobile, their backpacks full of food and wood to burn in the stove. And candles, of course, to cast shadows on the walls and across their bodies.

They were always careful to remove their traces.

Here, the lovers have not been so careful, knowing perhaps, in this town of only ten thousand, that the absentee owners were not likely to appear. Kate goes down the hall to the smaller bedroom with its small intact window spray-painted FUCK YOU in black. On the floor, a crude pentagram has been gouged into the linoleum.

The only furniture is an OKANAGAN APPLES box turned on end in the middle of the room, as if someone has used it to reach the light fixture, unscrew the bulb and take it away. This might have been Iris' or Elaine's room. Try as she might, Kate can't sense anything of either of them. They're too distant, too foreign to imagine here.

She brushes off the box and sits near the window. It's not quite noon, and the sun casts a backward UOY KCUF on the floor. She opens Elaine's sealed manila envelope and pulls out its contents. The papers are written in blue ink and describe particular events. Although addressed to Kate, they're ramblings, recollections that Elaine has had over the years, both about herself and about Iris when they were small.

Dear Kate,

I met your father in November 1965 in Vancouver. He was still married but was not with your mother, who had run off to Goa with a girlfriend a couple of months before. Your father phoned me because he had not heard from Iris and had no idea where she was. She had left him a goodbye note, but given no indication of where she was going. At the time, I didn't know either. It was only when she returned that she told us where she'd been. But that's another story and comes much later. Between November 1965 and March 1966, your father and I had a love affair, which ended when Iris returned in the spring and wanted to patch things up. Joe and I were in love, but we decided to give each other up, because Joe wanted the best for you. Back then, there weren't a whole lot of single dads around, and if Iris had wanted to make trouble, she could have taken you away. And Joe didn't want to give you up.

Elaine

One by one, Kate flips through the pages, looking for a letter in which Elaine explains herself and the reasons for the subterfuge, an apology. She sits there all afternoon. *Did Elaine really believe these dates and events would satisfy me? This isn't a background, a history. Too much is missing. Did Elaine intend my father to fill in the details? Does he even know what they are?* Then, mixed in with the letters, she finds a smaller envelope, the words IRIS AND ELAINE printed on its front. Inside are three photos of the two of them as young girls: side by side, clutching teddy bears; riding atop a parade float; and hugging at a bus station.

PHOTO #1: THE BETTER BEAR

September, 1952. Iris is six, Elaine nine. Both girls are wearing pleated skirts and cardigans, Iris' a bright orange, Elaine's green. They are clutching stuffed teddy bears their father brought home as gifts after a trip. Iris' bear is lifelike — a plush giant panda with creamy body and black ears, limbs and shoulders. Its soft marble eyes are ringed in black, giving it a mischievous appearance; Elaine's bear is brown, ordinary, its synthetic fur rough, its button eyes unexpressive.

When their father gave them the bears, Elaine swallowed several times, her pride forcing the lump back down her throat. Her bear was ugly, of poor quality, an afterthought, the type of gift someone buys in a hurry, without consideration. Her father saw her distress and took her aside to explain that he had only been able to find one panda and, had he given it to her, Iris would surely have cried. Because Elaine was older, her father said, she would understand if he gave Iris the better bear.

Elaine bit her lip and didn't cry. Iris named her panda The Better Bear.

Throughout their childhood, everyone treated Iris as if she were breakable. Partly this was because Iris was often ill, high-strung, unpredictable. One unkind word could send her off to her room, to lie in bed, head turned toward the wall, tears etching her cheeks. Elaine resented her sister immensely, convinced that Iris was manipulating them all with her histrionics. Later, in their teens, Iris often accused Elaine of being jealous of her because she was prettier, younger, because their father loved her more, because she always got the better bear.

... Years later, when our father no longer spoke to or about Iris, when none of us was allowed to mention her name

at home, Iris called me long-distance from Seattle. I could
hear boat horns and people laughing, even the sound of
the waves against the wharf. She was going to Goa, she
told me, her voice excited, manic. I asked her about you
and Joe, but Iris didn't want to talk about that. She wanted
me to promise that if anything happened to her, every-
thing of hers would go to you. When I agreed, she laughed
long and hard — not a humorous laugh either. "Poor
Elaine," she said. "You still don't get The Better Bear."

I know it's taken a long time for me to fulfill this
promise, Kate, but I always hoped Iris would return to
claim you. I have kept all her things for you. Your father
has them in the shed at the house.

PHOTO #2: PARADE

July 1st, Dominion Day, 1960. Iris and Elaine ride on a
float, wearing white sunglasses and identical dresses
made by their mother. Although this photo is black and
white, Kate imagines the emerald satin of a dress her
mother made for her doll when Kate was three or four.
Iris may have culled it from the dress she wore on the float
— a puffy waist-cincher whose modest bodice suggests
the swelling of breasts; the tiny spaghetti straps she could
manoeuvre off her shoulder with the slightest shrug, as
she had seen Suzanne Pleshette do in movies.

What is not recorded is the scene at the picnic
grounds after the parade, when one of her father's friends

corners her on a path and slides his hand up her leg, under the elastic of her underpants, his beer breath hot and stale at her neck. She slaps him off, runs away while he watches her, licking his fingers and laughing. What's not recorded is the moment hours later, in her bedroom, when her mother slaps her and calls her a liar. And even later, in the darkness, when her father calls her a slut.

PHOTO #3: GOODBYE

Bus station, 1962. The photo is taken on Elaine's Brownie camera by a stranger. Iris is about to step on the bus bound for Vancouver. The two of them are hugging. What you can't see are their wet cheeks, their trembling lips; what you can't hear are the whispered promises of letters and phone calls that their father intercepted for years.

Kate slides the photos into the small envelope, walks room to room, trying to imagine a family seated together at suppertime, listening to the radio on Sunday nights, laughing under a Christmas tree, shouting at each other through the locked bathroom door. It confuses her to meet Iris this way. How is it possible, she thinks, to be twelve one day, laughing and trustful, eyes adoring the same father who years later you leave behind, your memory of him shaped and reshaped until even you don't recognize him any more?

The ghosts linger.

Around four o'clock, when the sun drops behind the circle of mountains, and the air cools, she gathers everything, returns it to the envelope and drives back to town, her head filled with vignettes of Iris' life before she left home and met Joe and became her mother.

She calls Elaine's old lawyer and he lists her options:

1. abandon the property and let the back taxes accumulate until the city seizes it; or
2. find Iris and have her sign the appropriate papers; or
3. have Iris declared "Presumed to be dead," a complex legal procedure that requires extensive investigation, affidavits, lawyers, money and time.

Kate is confident she will find her. *Every contact leaves a trace.* Even extinct species leave trails — petrified hollows where feet once touched, ghost dwellings in cliffs or, underground, fragments of bones and shards of imagination.

Some time earlier, Kate became fascinated by Rachel Whiteread, a British sculptor whose installations are representations of space. She looked at photographs of her work, beginning with a full-size casting in plaster of the space within a closet. There are photos of the space inside objects, in and around humans, rooms. Photos of the casting of an entire house — sprayed in concrete from the inside, then laboriously disassembled brick by brick from the outside, so that all that remains is an *impression* of space. Absence solidified.

In the morning, she drives to Mt. Elizabeth Secondary School and looks through yearbooks until she finds the one in which her mother is in Grade 11.

The photos do not capture the chiaroscuro of Iris' personality. Kate stares at the shiny cheeks, the glossy pink lipstick, curled eyelashes and kohl-ringed eyes, the black bangs cut just below her eyebrows. Iris is smiling, her mouth turned up slightly more on one side than the other. Kate pulls out her driver's licence, puts it beside Iris' picture and studies their two faces for similarities. She's surprised to find so many — their hair, the shape of their chins, the curve of their shoulders. She stares at Iris' face until her eyes hurt .... The foundation of evolution ... *grandfather, grandmother, Iris, Dad, me* ... and of life itself is the transmission of genetic material ... *to flee* ... one generation to the next. Imprints. If someone could take cross-sections of our hearts, she thinks, they might find rosebuds.

After she has xeroxed every photo of Iris and all the pages in which the students in her grade appear, she returns to the hotel, takes out the phone book and matches names with numbers. She doesn't really expect anyone to know where Iris is, because the lawyer told her that no one answered the notices when her grandparents died.

Some people remember Iris but say they didn't know her very well. They refer Kate to others. She follows every lead and finally is rewarded by a woman's soft voice. "We were good friends for a while, Iris and me. It was a long time ago, though, you understand, and we were so young. I might have some things up in the attic … sure I remember this and that …."

Later, after supper, Kate is surprised by the middle-aged woman who answers the door. "Claire Rabelais," she says, pronouncing it "Rebellious."

Kate shakes her hand, realizing that Iris is fifty-one, not that fresh young face in the photographs. She could look just like Claire, squished into purple sweatpants and matching top, the extra twenty-five pounds all bunched around her waist and hips. She could live in a house just like this, with dark brown fake-panelled walls, yellow tweed shag rugs and an imitation-wood TV set. She might have a plaid couch and a La-Z-Boy and thick yellow drinking glasses that feel like plastic against your lips.

But the Iris Kate has imagined is forever young. Sleeping Beauty.

Claire motions Kate to the couch. She has spread papers all over the coffee table — photos and invitations and ticket stubs — things she has taken out of the box on the floor. She shows Kate handwritten programs for school plays they attended — *Hamlet, Othello*. "Iris thought that was the most romantic play, even though Desdemona got herself killed in the end." She has faded orange ticket stubs to movies they saw — *Voyage to the*

Bottom of the Sea, Cleopatra, Rome Adventure. "Troy Donahue was the sexiest man in the world!"

There are photos of them in bikinis at Kitimat River, Hirsch Creek. "We never swam, of course, the water was much too cold." She opens a box of girl-group records, the Supremes, the Chantels. "Iris and me, we wanted to be in a band right from the time we went to junior high," she says. "Iris played guitar and I'd taken a few piano lessons. We used to put those records on and sing along with them at the top of our lungs, until one of our parents came out and told us to can it." She laughs.

When Iris reached puberty, Claire tells Kate, most of her girlfriends at school enrolled in shorthand and home-ec classes; they were supposed to be interested in clothes, furniture and fruit canning. Nobody sat around cross-legged playing guitar and listening to Joan Baez like Iris did. Girls wore cute matching outfits and went to the hairdresser once a week. Iris sulked in black stovepipe pants and turtleneck sweaters, kohl-ringed eyes, raven hair swishing to her waist. Instead of *Bride* magazine she read *Rolling Stone*.

"Once she started all this, Iris became a bit of an outcast," Claire says. "Oh sure, the girls at school — me included — we thought she was pretty gutsy, but no one would have dared be like her. It would have embarrassed our families and decent boys wouldn't have asked us out. You can't imagine," Claire says, shaking her head, "how important all that was back then."

Kate concentrates, trying to tunnel through time, to excavate a past for herself, something to lean on, to try on.

"And look at this!" Claire exclaims, delighted. She hands Kate a cedar souvenir box.

Kate stares at the jumping fish on its lid, over which the words *Campbell River, B.C.* are scrolled in white italics. Inside the box, a rhinestone silver bracelet.

"That belonged to Iris," Claire says. "She gave it to me before she left for good. A keepsake ... you know ... it was precious to her. You take it."

Dear Kate,

When Iris was fifteen, she imagined herself in love. The man was years older and had no inkling of her devotion.

I don't remember who he was, exactly, but I think he was the brother of one of Mom's friends. He might have been called Roger. He'd come to work at Alcan Aluminum Smelter for the summer and was boarding with us. Mom moved Iris into my room and fixed up hers for him. He would have been in his mid-twenties, I think. This is partly hearsay, because I don't remember much of it, but Iris retold me the story when we were both adults, so who knows?

Anyway, Iris had this passion for him — undeclared, of course — and when he was at work, she used to sneak into his room and go through his things. She told me later that she didn't disturb anything; she simply gazed at his possessions, fingered things he'd touched … you know, romantic teenager stuff. Do you remember how you eloped when you were that age? The best Iris could do was to buy herself a diary that locked and every night make up a chapter of their love affair.

Naturally, no one knew that it was a fabrication, so when Mom decided to see just exactly what Iris was so intent on locking away, she got the shock of her life. First she told Father, then they confronted Iris, who denied it all. Mom wasn't convinced and insisted that Father question the young man, despite Iris' pleas. Of course Roger was mighty surprised himself and, while they were having a chat, Iris decided to kill herself. She didn't really know how to go about it, but she thought that seeing as she wasn't a very good swimmer, she would throw herself into Minette Bay and drown.

Minette Bay was a few miles out on a logging road, so the only way to get there was to hitch a ride. She stood at the side of the road for several hours and, when a friend of our parents stopped, he talked her out of it and drove her home instead.

Poor Roger had to board somewhere else. Iris was mortified. She moped around for the rest of the summer, and no one mentioned her "suicide attempt." Roger must have understood, or at least felt sorry for her, because when he returned home in the fall, he sent her a little box with a bracelet in it, and a note saying he hoped she was feeling better. Iris turned beet red, ripped up the note and swore she'd never wear the bracelet. But she kept it all the same.

Elaine

A memory surfaces and roots, triggered by the suggestion of Iris' past, as if Kate's mind were a camera, and memories the points of focus the lens chances upon. It reminds her of the film *Blowup*, of the possibilities within memory to record the unintentional. Logging road. Tree shapes. Water. A summer night when she was thirteen.

She'd been babysitting for Angie and her first husband, Brad. On the drive home, windows down, Brad flung his arm across the back of her seat. Perhaps he'd noticed the lingering looks she gave him when she went to the diner. He was twenty-one, handsome, older. She was infatuated, intoxicated by his lazy glances, his smiles.

When he turned off the highway onto a logging road, she didn't object. Her heart thumped in her chest; he was a spotlight aimed at her. She laughed with her mouth open, teeth perfectly aligned, imitating the lipstick models in *Vogue*. She blinked slowly and sultried him, lids at half-mast, as she'd seen movie stars do.

He stopped the car and turned off the motor. Then he

slid closer, and his fingers stroked her shoulder. "You're so pretty," he said. "I'll bet you've never been kissed."

She shook her head, her face flushed.

He reeled her to him and kissed her, forcing his tongue between her surprised lips. He tasted of alcohol and cigarettes, of parties and forbidden things. While he kissed her, his hand undid the buttons of her blouse so quickly and expertly she was unaware he'd done it until he moved away from her, and she saw her white cotton Playtex bra. She tried to pull her shirt shut, but he murmured, "Beautiful. Beautiful," and she was captivated by the tone, the awe, by her sudden power, her senses awakened. He undid her bra, then cupped her breast. In one quick movement, he lifted her onto his lap and buried his face in her breasts, his mouth at her nipples. She didn't know where to put her hands, what to do. He began to press himself hard against her, his eyes feverish and distant. *Repulsion, attraction, curiosity, fear.* She pulled away from him and he sighed.

"No one's ever done that, huh?" he said, as he leaned over and touched her cheek.

She flinched. "I want to go home," she said, staring out the window.

In front of the house, he took out his wallet and counted out the babysitting money. Then he added an extra five dollars. She felt sick to her stomach, threw the bill back at him and ran up the steps.

Joe was waiting for her as usual. She forced herself to

smile, to walk slowly past him upstairs to the bathroom where she scrubbed her chest and brushed and flossed her teeth and put on her long flannel nightgown. She examined her face carefully: although she did not look different, everything had changed.

On her journey south through B.C., Kate stops at every city and town library to check for Iris' name in the phone books. She searches for both *Hinton*, Iris' maiden name, and *Mason*, her married one. Not only are both names common, but in all likelihood, Iris has remarried and changed her name again. Kate can't imagine her living alone. When did Dad divorce her? She'll ask him when she gets home.

Terrace, Smithers, Prince George, Quesnel, Kamloops, Kelowna, Vernon, Osoyoos.

She writes down the phone numbers for I. Hintons and Masons, and phones them. No one knows Iris.

Across the border. Omak, Okanogan. Then, instead of turning left the few miles to Twisp, she is propelled south on Highway 17, on a hunch, foot on the gas, the road a persistent seduction.

Bridgeport. Soap Lake. Grant Orchards. Then, Moses Lake, where she logs on at the library computer to do an Internet phone and address search. Three Iris Masons — one in Indiana, one in Kentucky and one in Illinois. She jots down the phone numbers and addresses, then posts a message on a Missing Persons Newsgroup:

Anyone knowing the whereabouts of Iris
Mason, née Hinton, Canadian-born, and who
lived in Twisp, Washington, from 1962 to 1967,
please contact Kate Mason on a very urgent
family matter.

She types her phone number and her father's, her street
and e-mail address. Then she searches cities in B.C. and
Washington State whose populations exceed thirty
thousand, finds the largest newspaper in each and, using
a credit card, places notices. From a pay phone outside
the library in Moses Lake, she calls the Irises in Indiana,
Kentucky and Illinois, but they are names only and have
no connection to her.

It is now late afternoon, ninety-one degrees, the
ground brown and dusty except for the verdant green
around the lake. She decides to spend the night here and
go to Twisp in the morning. *I must call Dad. I must call
Rose.* She searches for a motel she stayed in years ago, but
everything has changed, the town grown, modernized.
As she drives past the airport with its 747s taxiing on and
off the runways, she wonders if Iris got on a plane and
crossed an ocean or two. Trained as a flight attendant
and lived in the air. Stowed away, perhaps, to Japan,
Egypt. She could be anywhere.

I must ask Dad why Iris went to Goa.

She checks into a motel on the lake, next to a bar
where she eats dinner. She brings a notebook and,

between bites, jots down questions for Dad and Rose and Angie. She keeps asking herself: What's missing?

Finally, when she can avoid it no longer, she goes back to her room and phones her father.

"Is Angie there with you?"

He sighs loudly, as if he intends her to hear he's fed up. "Where are you now?" he asks.

"Is anything you've ever said true?" It's as if they're speaking to each other, but the moment the words escape their mouths they are deadened by air, like rocks are by water when they break the ocean's surface.

He sighs again, loudly. "Rose is worried about you."

"You might get a call or two about Iris," she says. "I've been putting notices in the papers." She pauses. "I'll be back tomorrow sometime."

She hangs up and phones Rose.

"Kate, I've been waiting for you to call," Rose says.

"Yeah. Well."

"Your dad says you're looking for Iris."

"So?" She tries to keep her voice casual.

"Well, I was around some of the time, and Elaine told me things ... for you to know later ...."

"Is it later enough?" Kate says, her voice edgy.

"I'm really sorry, Kate." Her voice is genuine, pleading.

"Yeah. Well," Kate says.

~

Imagine this: a father takes his favourite daughter, dresses her in the finest clothes, kisses her goodbye and sends her off to a mountaintop to die of exposure and starvation. The purpose? Eternal life for him. Two-thousand years later, there she is, frozen stiff and perfectly preserved. In his mind, she is forever young, forever walking toward the sacrificial altar, head held high, proud even to be the vehicle of her father's transcendence from mortal to god. The Inca's Capacocha Ritual.

Of course, her skull is broken, implying she's been mercy-killed before being walled into her mountain grave; implying the high priests knew there was nothing glorious about this death, except, perhaps, ritual and faith.

~

Father hood, father figure, holy father, fatherland, fathership, father time, fatherless.

She's not home ten minutes when Angie arrives in her mint-green cotton sweater and microfiber pants, all smiles and *too familiar*. It's as if Angie spent the morning hidden up the street, watching for Kate's car, and now is trying to act surprised to see her.

"Did you have a good trip?" she says. "Any news? How was the weather?" all without waiting for Kate to answer. "What was the lawyer like? Will you sell the property?"

"I don't know," Kate says, answering all the questions at once.

Angie brings a carful of empty boxes, which she cheerfully unloads onto the porch, and starts house-cleaning — "Let me help with this, Joe .... Why don't you let me handle that?" — as if she were entitled to make decisions for him, for them. Kate stands by, mute, hands clenching and unclenching. *I'm still here*, she wants to shout. *Can't you see me?* Bile rises in her throat and she swallows several times, then stomps into the kitchen where she pours herself a double scotch and slams the freezer door when she replaces the ice tray.

"We've got to go through Elaine's things, choose what to keep and send the rest to the Sally Ann," Angie informs her casually.

Kate keeps her eyes averted, her lips close to the glass. She stares through the liquid distortion into that other time. Did Elaine do this with Kate's things when Kate was sent to live with Rose? There must have been many closets and chests filled with treasures — her entire childhood boxed and taped by a stranger. Did Elaine read Kate's diaries, listen to her Foreigner tapes, anguish over Brink's *An Instant in the Wind*, try on her miniskirts, laugh at her drawings, untie the letters she wrote to an absent mother? *This is our house.*

Angie shepherds Kate's father room to room.

Kate pours a second drink, picks up a book she's been reading on extinction and survival, and flees to the porch.

84

She can't totally ignore the hustle and bustle inside, the full boxes, which, periodically, either Angie or Joe stack to one side of the porch. CLOTHES, the marker proclaims, or SHOES or PERSONAL. It makes her want to rush to Vancouver and label all her things so that no one can possibly misinterpret her life, set up a grid of her apartment and catalogue everything as if it were an archeological dig. Angie and Joe are missing the most crucial part in the interpretation of Elaine's life — the location of the objects in relationship to one another or to Elaine herself.

Somebody lived and died here, she wants to shout at them. But their goal is to cram the past into boxes and send it away. Leave the house cleared, airy, ready to receive the present.

As Joe and Angie bustle around her, she begins to feel like an inanimate object they will, at any moment, stuff into a box and label TROUBLESOME DAUGHTER. She fights the urge to do it herself.

When Angie comes out with a plastic bag filled with Elaine's clothes, Kate is reminded of the quilt. She imagines Elaine curved over the table for hundreds of hours, choosing fabrics, cutting them into perfect tiny squares, arranging them by colour and design, carefully writing out the instructions.

"Don't touch the quilt pieces in my room," she says to Angie. "I'll take care of that."

Angie flushes. "I just want to help —"

"Fuck off," Kate says. "Don't go playing Little Miss

Helpful around me. I *know* you."

Angie stares at her as if Kate were a stranger. Joe, who has witnessed this from the doorway, steps onto the porch. Kate keeps her eyes cold and small, until Angie turns and runs to her car. Joe follows her and soothes her through the open car window.

Go-o-o-o-o-ne, go-o-o-o-o-ne, go-o-o-o-o-ne. With each repetition, Kate regresses until she is two years old, in Rose's house, casting her toys into corners, behind drapes, under beds, couches, chairs, in the small space between counter and fridge. "*Go-o-o-o-o-ne!*" she says, and claps her hands as she disposes of each. When Rose stops buying her new toys, Kate hurls knick-knacks, matchbook covers, lipstick, eyeliner, apples, plums — anything that fits in her hand. "*Go-o-o-o-ne,*" she squeals.

Now and then, however, she reaches into the closet corner or behind the washing machine and pulls out a small car, a yellow building block, some forgotten pleasure, and exclaims loudly and joyfully, "There! There!"

She looks up when she hears her father's boots on the stairs. She expects he will reprimand her, and she'll have to fight him too. She stares at the cover of her book, *Extinction and Survival in Human Populations.* Instead, her father sits, quiet, on the top step, for what seems like an eternity. She can almost pretend they are back to when it was just the two of them. She was always so afraid to upset him, terrified that he would cast her away.

Of course, he did.

"When did you get divorced?" she asks, finally.

He's startled by her question. "Late Seventies?" he says, vague.

"You must have known where Iris was then," she says. "Where was I? Why didn't you ever say anything?"

Her father slumps as if someone had put a heavy sack around his neck. He rubs his forehead repeatedly, his eyes staring at a distant horizon. She leans her elbows on her knees, hands under her chin, and waits.

"I didn't know where she was," he says presently. "I forged her signature on the documents." He stares at her, eyes unflinching.

"But surely that's illegal," she says, her voice childlike and whiny.

"Elaine and I wanted to get married. It was the simplest thing."

"You and Elaine had yourselves a good time, didn't you?" she says, bitter. "Made fools of everyone."

"Kate, it wasn't like that."

She stares into space, kicking her foot against the railing — *thump, thump, thump* — until it irritates even her. In a little over a week, her father has managed to turn what she remembers of her life here into a facade. "What else?" she says. "Tell me all of it now." When he doesn't answer, she asks, "Did you ever love my mother?"

"More than you can imagine," he says. "Why do you think I took her back even after she'd been gone overseas a year ...."

"Elaine said you fell in love with *her*. That my mother meant nothing to you."

"Elaine is wrong," he says firmly. "I'm not saying I didn't care for Elaine, but the moment Iris came home ...." He shakes his head. "There's never been anyone else, not really."

She looks up and the sky is an opaque layer stars burn through, a gauze receding into black. *Celestial bodies*, she thinks, imagining angels. She can't recall a sky so dense with stars.

Suddenly, her father reaches for her hand in the darkness. "Your mother," he says, his voice barely above a whisper, "she liked to sit here at night, in summer."

Kate holds still, afraid even a breath might break the spell of his voice, filled with emotions she's never heard before. She squeezes his hand.

"Iris claimed she could *hear* the night. Not just the sounds of night, you understand, but something else ... something that spoke to her ...."

The sound of loneliness, Kate thinks, of solitude.

"In the shed," he says, "your mother's things." He slips a key between their joined hands.

She lies in bed, the key on the bedside table, and listens to familiar morning father-sounds: water spattering the shower curtain, bare feet padding down the hall, coffee perking, bacon splattering, the door latching shut. She waits until she hears wheels scrape gravel before she gets up, makes fresh coffee, then goes out to the shed. She takes with her a spiral notebook in which to record everything, five blank file folders from her father's office, a felt marker, a pair of scissors, a hole puncher and a ball of string.

The shed has always been Joe's sanctuary, off limits to Kate. In fact, it's not a shed but part of the basement that's been sealed off and can only be accessed from outside. It's been there as long as Kate can remember. She assumes her father built the barrier wall after Iris left.

When she steps inside, she's surprised to find it warm. Joe has piped in a heating vent. There are two small rooms. The first is a workshop: tools hang on the walls; red Sears Mastercraft toolboxes are stacked on the floor, their drawers full of screws, nails, washers and other small objects she doesn't recognize; tires and garden implements lean against a post; and terra-cotta flowerpots nest inside one another in a corner, next to a collapsible ladder. She walks past them all to the second room in the back, which is barely larger than a closet.

Under a thick mantle of dust and spider webs she finds: two trunks and three sewing boxes, a six-string guitar in its case, a pair of cowboy boots, a hardboard wardrobe, a rusted turquoise bicycle, a faded blue-velvet hatbox inside of which is a panda bear, a black salesman suitcase, a saddle, a doll in a baby carriage, a pair of stilts and an old tin of Mixed Fruit Drops — a souvenir of the coronation of Queen Elizabeth II — which contains a garnet ring.

She stares at this evidence of her mother and memories flash like a music video, incoherent, disjointed: tickle, pink angora against her face, Iris' white teeth, red lips, octaves of laughter, falling, the slippery railing of a bridge, giddy nausea as she whirls with Iris on the porch, roaring water on stones, winter night drive, Iris in a flimsy nightgown, bare feet, startled eyes .... She forces herself to think about archeological digs — Albertan dinosaurs, Egyptian mummies, Etruscan necropolises — the distance needed, the order, the attention to detail.

She takes a deep breath, makes her mind a slate and begins. She unravels the string and marks off the back room into sixteen squares. After she has secured the ends, she sits down and draws the grid into her notebook, filling in the items in each quadrant.

1	2	3	4
	SEWING BOX 1	SEWING BOX 3	TRUNK 1 & 2
5 SADDLE & BOOTS	6 SALESMAN SUITCASE	7 VELVET HATBOX & THE BETTER BEAR	8 HARDBOARD WARDROBE
9	10 SEWING BOX 2	11 BABY CARRIAGE & DOLL	12 GUITAR
13 STILTS	14 TURQUOISE BICYCLE	15	16 MIXED FRUIT DROP TIN & GARNET RING

When she has finished recording everything, she cuts up the file folders into three-by-two-inch cards, punches a hole in the corner of each, slips through a piece of string. She wonders how many of these things were stored here by Iris and how many her father added after she left. These are Iris' rejects, what she didn't want to take to her new life. She ties the first label to the handle of the guitar and, in felt pen, writes the item and the quadrant number: GUITAR [12].

She brushes off the dust before opening the case. The inside is lined in yellow crushed velvet, worn in one corner. The guitar is a rich reddish brown, with a fan of hairline cracks near the sound hole. Glued to the inside is a label:

SILVERTONE
MODEL NO. 26954
SIMPSON–SEARS LIMITED
MADE IN JAPAN

She slowly lifts the guitar and takes it outside to the porch where she sits and strums the old strings, even though they're stretched out of tune. She's summoning a memory, in perfect pitch, like one might rub a lantern to conjure a genie. If she concentrates hard enough, she can hear Iris here on the porch; she can recall the silk of her ebony hair, the warmth of her arm, the rich contralto of her voice.

GUITAR [12]

In Kate's grandparent's house, in northern B.C., it was forbidden to speak Iris' name and had been since 1962, the year Joan Baez sold more records than any other female folksinger in history, the year Iris ran away from home to become a folksinger/songwriter herself. She had spent the previous six months sitting in her room, decked in black skinny pants, turtleneck sweater and pointy flats (which she'd ordered from the Simpson-Sears catalogue and paid for with her babysitting money), listening to folk music and writing socially-conscious lyrics about thalidomide babies and the evils of conservative parents.

She wanted to be a beat poet, a novelist, a folksinger, somebody somewhere else. She wanted to be a freedom fighter, an advocate for world peace. At night, she tuned her shortwave to distant stations, stirred by the immense world beyond Kitimat. Out there, young people her age were championing civil rights. Iris was impatient for things to happen; she heard a call to arms. Barely sixteen, she packed her clothes into a green leatherette bag, her song lyrics into a black cardboard salesman's case with the words MIAMI BARBER COLLEGE stenciled on the top, and her acoustic guitar into its soft vinyl case, and rode a bus out of Kitimat, toward her new life in the city.

After a nine-hundred-mile trip, Iris arrived in Vancouver. She immediately bought a newspaper, rented a room in a rambling house and landed a job in a small book-store. In her spare time, she hung out on 4th Avenue, played her guitar, smoked marijuana and slept with a succession of young men, convinced that free love would save the environment, stop wars, eliminate crime and create Utopia.

When her father comes home, it's past eleven and Kate's no longer angry with Angie. She has spent the evening sewing Elaine's quilt. The work has kept her mind occu-pied, so that she has not been able to think of anything but the precision of her stitches, the positioning of each square in relation to others. She has begun to imagine that the squares form a grid, a Picasso narrative made up of the arbitrary fragments of Elaine's life story.

"Dad?" she calls when she hears his steps on the stairs.

He stops in the doorway. "You're finishing the quilt," he says.

He has read the instructions. She holds up the six-by-seven-inch rectangle she's working on. "It takes forty-two pieces to make this," she says. "All different fabrics, too. It must have taken her forever to cut them."

"It was her hobby," her father says. "She made quilts for everyone."

"Perhaps her life was falling apart," Kate says slowly. "Perhaps this was her way of putting it back together."

When she and Stephen broke up, she went to a hobby store and bought herself balsa-wood model kits — aero-planes, ships, submarines, tanks — which she spent the next six months constructing. By the time she'd amassed a small army in the corner of her apartment, Stephen had stopped calling and the war was over. She took the models to a secluded beach along English Bay, built a fire on the rocks and fed in the models one by one. The balsa exploded into flames, then just as quickly crumpled into itself, into black, fragile ash.

She holds up the square again. "Look. It does make a lovely new thing," she says. "But the patterns — the lights and darks, at least — only match if you move away." She pauses. "And all the seams show."

Her father stands motionless.

She bends her head over the fabric, keeps her hands busy so he can't see them waver.

When he leaves abruptly, she doesn't know how to call him back. She hears him rummaging through drawers in his bedroom, then he returns with a small, purple-velvet jewellery box, which he opens and holds out to her. Inside, is a jet choker and a brass ankle bracelet of tiny bells. Fit for a gypsy.

GYPSY ANKLET [FROM DAD]

The first time Joe saw Iris, she was standing on the corner of 4th and Cypress, in a flowing white dress cinched under the breasts with a rope in a Grecian criss-cross, Indian sandals on her feet, playing guitar in a jug band. He fell in love with her immediately. He was twenty-five, on a three-day holiday, and had never been in love. Except for his police training, he had never left Twisp. Two months earlier, his parents had moved to Phoenix, leaving him the family home. This was his first adventure, his first hitchhike to Vancouver where his sister, Rose, lived.

He didn't speak to Iris that day, only watched her, mesmerized, and put coins in her open guitar case. He stared at her milky skin and lustrous hair, at the faint areolae of her nipples against the white fabric, at her laced, sandalled feet. She noticed him, of course; how could she ignore his corduroy pants and Hush Puppies, his military haircut and shy smile.

On the second day, when he stepped off the bus, they made awkward small talk.

He spent his last morning in Chinatown, searching for an appropriate gift to give her before he left. He found the brass anklet shimmering on a street vendor's blanket. That afternoon, when Joe presented the anklet, Iris held out her foot for him to secure the clasp, then twirled round and round so that the bells jingled in rhythm to the band's music.

Early evening, in Rose's car, he scooped Iris from her rooming house downtown and took her to see *Lolita*. Afterwards, they drove to Jericho Beach, past the military barracks, and parked facing the water. She pulled him, laughing, out of the car, her thick black hair brushing his arms; made him chase her into the flats of the low tide. She slowly undid the rope belt, pushed the dress off her shoulders and ran into the water. He could hear her laughter, his name being called over and over. He undressed quickly and followed her in. The water was cold but shallow when he reached her, thankful for the camouflage of night. She fluttered around him, graceful and fluid, so that his hands never quite touched her; his lips never quite grazed hers. Finally she led him out of the water, and they fell into each other with a dizzying hunger.

Naturally, Joe didn't tell Kate all of this; he drew a modest curtain after Iris undressed. Kate foraged her own memory bank. *Ray*. Mexican beach. The water warm. Christmas — one of the few she has enjoyed.

In Kate's memories, Iris is much more ambiguous — sometimes barefoot, laughing on the porch, with Kate in her arms like a miniature dance partner; other times the sting of her voice could plunge Kate into hysterical anxiety. She wonders what her father meant to tell her — that Iris' coming and leaving had only to do with sex? Or was he describing something intangible, the beginning of their romance, his capacity to love?

Then a car up the drive, a knock. Kate looks out the window and sees Rose. She forces herself to stay in her room while her father goes downstairs. Rose's voice wafts up to her, a vapour of calm settling around Kate's heart. Joe's footsteps pound on the stairs. He knocks at her door. "Kate? Rose is here to see you." He returns to his room and shuts the door.

Kate goes downstairs, and there is Rose, eyes enlarged with tears, pink silk shawl rustling. "How are you, my darling?" she says when she sees Kate. "I came as soon as I could."

Rose is a young Bette Davis — thick black pageboy and deep-set blue eyes. She's fifty-six and willowy thin, the latter maintained by salads and three hours of aerobics a week. She's been divorced for as long as Kate remembers, and has no children. When she's not listening to Kate's woes, she's busy with Active Artists, a management company for rock groups — a job that keeps her in the air as much as on the ground.

Kate hugs her tight, despite wanting to be angry at her. Here they are for the first time, adults, in her mother's kitchen. Rose pulls out a chair and sits down as naturally as if she's always lived here. Rose and Iris must have sat in this kitchen and talked. Did Iris occupy a particular place? A special chair? Did she sit here and tell a girlfriend about her plans to flee? Once Kate did an online search for the word "vanish" and found a message entitled: *Plans To Vanish.* A young man wrote:

    I am planning trip to South East Asia and want
    to leave in spring. I'm going to cut ties to all
    my family and friends. I need to begin again.

97

A follow-up message read:

Have been gone 12 years. Regret it. Think,
plan, prepare financially & emotionally.

Both messages were two years old. Had these messages been pleas for intervention?

"Eddie someone-or-other has been calling for you," Rose says when Kate has poured them each a drink. "I didn't know whether to tell him where you were."

Kate waves her hand. Eddie is her last revolving-door affair. "He's ... an ex," she says, sitting at the table, then sighs, collapsing her head on her arms. *Poor Eddie. It wasn't his fault.* For a moment, she imagines every man she has ever hurt standing in front of her, on therapists' orders, come to confront her. What could she say to make them all feel better? To make herself feel better? Either/or. "He must feel awful," she says.

"I'd say he was a hysterical response to the divorce," Rose says.

Kate shrugs. Rose waits for her to elaborate, but Kate is well-practised at enunciations, omissions, transitions, modulations. She's like the Yanomami of the Amazon who refuse to call anyone by his or her real name lest they alert bad spirits to that person's whereabouts. *Ray,* she thinks, but she doesn't say it.

The exact reason she moved out is that, while cleaning out her apartment locker to make room for Eddie's bike, she found a box of her wedding photos. One memory led to another like a sentimental merry-go-round, then a drinking binge, a diazepam weekend and, finally, a goodbye wave from the rental truck in which she piled her possessions and drove to a new apartment.

"*1997: Kate hysterical*," Rose says in the voice reserved for their game.

They've been doing this for years, scouring newspapers for discoveries, wars, achievements, deaths — anything they believe has historical value. They also note personal events and, on New Year's Eve, the two of them pick the top three — global and personal — to define that particular year. Then they commit them to memory. This tradition began twenty years ago, and stems from Rose's belief that her great-grandfather died of Alzheimer's. She's determined to use her memory as a talisman against a similar fate. The list spans the last three decades and, even now that they don't live together, they maintain it.

"1968," one of them might say.

"The fatal shootings of Martin Luther King and Robert Kennedy; the Chicago 8, the Democratic Convention; the Newport Folk Festival ... Jimi Hendrix ... Janis Joplin ...."

"Not hysterical," Kate says now. "Surprised. Disappointed. Betrayed." She stares at Rose, daring her to contradict her.

"I'm not going to keep apologizing, Kate," Rose says, matter-of-fact. "I have loved you as much as I could ever love anyone."

Tension rises like a squall in the waters of Georgia Strait. The two women sit side by side, Kate wrapped in a satin forest-green dressing gown, Rose in black pants, white turtleneck, pink shawl. They do not look at each other, smile, laugh or embrace. Kate focuses on the fingernail of the index finger of her left hand. She picks near the cuticle, lifts scabs of nail polish, which she flicks onto the table. Rose waits, silent, until Kate's index fingernail is completely bare. Then she says, "How was the trip up north?"

Kate sighs, and it sounds like an oxygen tank emptying. She squeezes Rose's hand and tells her about Elaine's notes, about the treasures in the shed she can't wait to sort through.

"Why don't you wait until you find her?" Rose says. "Go through her things *with* her."

Kate looks up, startled. "Preparation," she says. "I want to know a bit about her before I see her."

Rose raises her eyebrows. "That stuff goes back a long time. People change."

"Day to day, maybe," Kate says. "Not their character."

Rose shakes her head. "I'm not sure about that. If a stranger examined the boxes in my basement, I'll bet he'd come up with someone different."

"He wouldn't," Kate says, annoyed. "What do you think my work is about? How do you think we know what we know about all the civilizations before us?"

Rose smiles. "We think we know. Who's to say, really?"

"Science. This isn't guesswork."

"Or maybe it is — systemized guesswork."

"I give up," Kate says. "You're hopeless."

Rose leans back in her chair until the two front legs lift off the floor. "You OK for money?" she asks.

"I got a bit saved up," Kate tells her. "And a contract coming up in November." She'll have to hustle to set up something for spring. Next summer, she can work the cruise ships again.

"If you're planning to stay here a while," Rose says, "why don't you give up your apartment and move your stuff into my basement? Save some money."

Kate shakes her head. She's not sure how long it'll take to find Iris, or whether she even needs to be in Twisp to do it. What she does need though, is the possibility of privacy, the knowledge that she has somewhere to go that's hers alone. "Thanks anyway." She stands up and reaches for the bottle of scotch.

Rose watches her pour each of them another drink. "It's not all romantic, Kate."

Kate looks up. "What do you mean?"

"Iris. The things Elaine left for you ... they're about a child. I just don't want you to romanticize it all."

Kate thinks of Elaine's stories, the papers and envelopes. A paper chase. Once she was hired to track an employee's movements by looking through a box of his receipts. It's astounding how easily a life can be reconstructed. She followed him from grocery stores to gas stations to movies to hotels to bank machines, gambling casinos, you name it. Using a credit card is like leaving a contrail.

She takes a long swig of her scotch, then looks at Rose. "I'm a grown-up," she says. "Why don't you tell me whatever it is."

BEER COASTERS: TRUNK #1 [4]

When Iris woke up one morning at the age of seventeen, married and with a small baby, she realized that she might as well be living at home with her parents. It was 1963 and all around, a cultural explosion. Folksingers — in the largest numbers since the Civil War era — were singing about police dogs, racial murders. Peter, Paul & Mary's voices were blowing in the wind. Bob Dylan predicted that *The Times They Are A-Changin'*. The only things changing for Iris were those associated with child rearing. She had no friends. Once, she called her mother, who cried on hearing her voice, but told her, tearfully, that her father would not allow her to come home, not now.

Iris couldn't imagine herself parading up and down Main Street with a stroller, or going to bake sales and church picnics. What began as an afternoon out at the bar here and there, soon became evenings out, hired babysitters and secret rendezvous. It wasn't long before everyone knew. By the time Kate was one, Iris was picking up men in these same bars — often tourists passing through — to drink with until someone called Joe to come and get her.

In Kate's mind, the countless faces of her own one-night stands begin to flip, like pages turning, features altering, one man morphing into the other. She closes her eyes and sees her convocation, the surprise when she looked out from the stage and saw her father and Elaine seated beside Rose. *Ten years.* She walked back to her seat, degree in hand, her heart like an abscess in her chest. Once up the aisle, she took off her cap and gown and escaped to the Grad Centre, where she phoned for a taxi that took her downtown to The Town Pump, where she drank too much and danced too wildly till closing time, then went to the apartment of the bass player of a mediocre band, pulled out the condom she kept in the black velvet pouch that came with the gold chain her father had sent her, and had safe sex in the eerie, flickering light of CNN.

Rose watches her.

Kate puts her glass down. "But why did Dad put up with it?"

"He adored her." Rose shakes her head. "Iris was trying to self-destruct. Perhaps she wanted your dad to kick her out and she was trying to provoke him. Who knows? But he was so ashamed." She gets up, abruptly, and goes to the window, her back to Kate. "I think he sensed she was not well and this made him even more protective of her. In fact, it probably made her feel utterly suffocated."

In the morning, by the time Kate gets up and showers, it's almost eleven, and Rose has gone back to Vancouver. Kate drives to Angie's, thinking she'll have lunch there — an olive branch.

The sky is a royal blue, and it could be summer, except for the golds and yellows on the hillsides, a collage of fall she wishes she could paint. This is not one of her talents — or perhaps, as Rose said, she didn't devote the time to learn the craft of art, like she did of music. As a child, when Kate heard Iris had been a musician, she pestered Joe into buying her a piano. She remembers hundreds of hours spent practising scales, up and down the keyboard, her hands like small animals running in an enclosed space. Later, in her teens, she took up guitar and practised until the fingertips of her left hand were calloused and anaesthetized to the constant pressure against strings, until the nails of her picking fingers — the second and third finger of her right hand — stopped growing. Even now that she hardly plays, those two nails continue to break in the same place. Our bodies, she thinks, are conditioned to flinch in the right places at the right moments. Pavlovian.

She turns into the lot and parks under the sign. All around, a small army of cranes, tractors and graders manoeuvre this way and that — mechanical arms lift, dig, giant rollers pound the earth flat — the noise, obnoxious and deafening when she steps out of the car. She inches past obstacles, walks under a swinging concrete tube suspended by ropes in the hook of the crane. Someone motions her out of the way.

She goes first to the trailer to see if Patti's home, but there's no answer to her knock, and neither Trevor's car nor Patti's motorcycle is out front.

She cuts across to the diner and, when she opens the door, the chimes announce her entrance. It's too early for lunch; a lone man sits in a far booth and reads the paper. Angie comes in from the back room, sees her and nods her onto a stool.

"Coffee?" she says.

Kate nods. "I'm sorry about yesterday ...," she begins, but Angie waves her words away.

"It's all right. It's forgotten." Her lips curl into a lopsided smile.

It's not really forgotten, Kate thinks, but she smiles back anyway, relieved. True friendship, she thinks, is about manoeuvring around potholes. When the highway's paved and smooth, it's easy to travel, responses automatic, inattentive. She and Angie neglect each other: a letter here, a phone call there. Frivolous talk about work, holidays, this man or that. But the slightest strife funnels them into each other. For example, when Ray and Kate split up, Angie drove to the coast to see her, and not once did she say, "I told you so," either in word or gesture, although she had tried. If only it were possible to heed advice, Kate thinks, it would save everyone immense time. She imagines one of those statistics, like the number of years one sleeps in a lifetime. *Kate Mason has wasted twelve years of her life by not heeding advice.*

She sighs and holds up her coffee mug. Angie pours her a refill. Kate watches her, thinking how capable she is, how confident and casual Angie is inside her body. She stares out the window, wondering if Iris was anything like Angie, when she sees Trevor drive up and park. BLACK JEANS, WHITE T, STUDDED LEATHER JACKET. *Jimmy Dean costume.* PASTY SKIN, FURROWED BROW, SCOWL. *Patti,* Kate thinks, aware of her own failing.

"About time," Angie mutters.

Trevor ignores her, and slams into the kitchen, café door swinging on its hinges.

"Lunch is at twelve not one," Angie says.

Kate watches Trevor framed in the large square opening: he washes his hands, puts on an apron and flips the rotating circle of pegs mounted on the wall. He has a nasty gash on his cheek that makes him look like a two-bit hoodlum.

"I've been looking for Patti," she says. "Any idea where she is?"

He smirks. "You're asking me? Last I saw her, she was packing a suitcase."

She must have talked to her father, Kate thinks, flustered that Ray might be on his way. "Did she say anything about her dad?"

"Nope. Said she was going with you."

"With me?" Kate says, startled.

Trevor stares at her. "You tell her 'good riddance' from me," he says. He turns his back and begins lunch preparations, slams pots on the counter.

Kate looks at Angie, questioning, but Angie rolls her eyes and shakes her head, turns on the radio and scans rhythmic samplings of talk, jazz, country, rock, evangelists — all interrupting each other. Finally she flicks a switch and shoves in a Mariah Carey CD. She pours them another coffee, then resets the salt and pepper shakers side by side, folds and refolds a napkin. Picks up a Mexican ceramic jug — smiling sunflower on blue background — and pours cream into her coffee again.

Kate watches, her own anxiety growing. Suddenly Angie turns and accidentally knocks the jug onto the floor.

"Fuck!" She leaps up to get a broom and cloth.

"You may as well tell me," Kate says, keeping her face and voice perfectly controlled. "I'd rather hear it from you."

Angie turns to her, startled. "What?"

"You and Dad."

Angie stares at her for a moment, then bursts into laughter. "Is that what this is about?" She shakes her head. "You must be kidding."

Kate combs her fingers through her hair at the temples,

stares into her coffee. *You're supposed to be my friend.*

"Kate." Angie sits on the stool beside her. "I swear on a stack of Bibles ...." She puts her arm around Kate in a friendly gesture, but when Kate doesn't reciprocate, it begins to feel like a heavy weight around Kate's neck. They continue to listen to the song until, at precisely 12:30, all the ruckus outside ends, abruptly, and men swarm out of the cabs of the machinery, like crawling insects during a Raid spray. The sudden silence is startling. On the CD, Mariah is in the middle of a blues lick, her voice too loud. Angie gets up and quickly adjusts the volume. Kate thinks about sound, how it's deadened by bodies and alive in an empty room. She thinks about the complexity of speech, the ability of flesh to become thick blotter, how we can achieve true clarity when no one is listening.

"Did I tell you Ray's got himself a Mexican girlfriend?" Angie says between lunch orders. "Sounds serious." She turns her back, takes a ham-and-cheese sandwich from under the glass dome, peels off the cellophane wrap and slides it into the microwave. "That's why he didn't come back this year."

Kate keeps her body perfectly still. "Poor Patti," she says. "Doesn't take much for him to push her down the list." Despite her concentration, Ray appears at the edge of her consciousness in an image borrowed from a Caribbean cruise ad she saw last week. Night beach, full moon, swaying palms filled with fairy lights, and there he is, smiling, laughing, his hands stroking the hair of a beautiful Mexican girl. On the horizon, the ship moves back and forth, a glittering castle, with row upon row of tiny lit windows. She presses her fingers into her temples and the vision recedes. Only a gnawing pain remains in the pit of her stomach. She searches her purse, takes out three antacid tabs and chews them quickly.

After the lunch crowd thins out, Angie calls Trevor to the front, then motions Kate to follow her into the living quarters.

The baby is fast asleep in her crib in the middle of the living room, where the coffee table used to be.

Angie sighs and collapses onto the couch. "Looks like Patti's *really* gone ... I didn't think much of it at first," she says. "I assumed she'd gone off with some friend ...." She picks lint off her sleeve.

"How long has she been missing?" Kate asks.

"A week ... since the funeral."

A whirling begins in Kate's ears, like a swarm of starlings. She stares at the crib, at the pink, pudgy face. *Déjà-vu.* "I just don't believe Patti would leave the baby behind," she says. "Did you report her missing?"

"She's not missing," Angie says, annoyed. "Her motorcycle's gone."

"I said I'd help her," Kate says. "She wasn't going anywhere without that baby."

"Well, she did." Angie pauses. "Kate, you of all people ought to know that women can, and do, abandon their babies."

~

Memories of discarded babies prowl the earth, spectres waiting to be found. Sometimes, it takes years: the butterbox babies — newborns discovered decades later buried in butter boxes in the walls of a Nova Scotia convent; sometimes months: "The small happiness," as the Chinese call a baby girl in a country where, each year, tens of thousands of female infants are abandoned in orphanages; sometimes weeks: the sixteen-year-old who escaped from the Japanese whorehouse into which her mother had sold her to support a gambling habit; sometimes days: the newborn dumped in the trash by the teenager who gave birth in the girls' washroom at her senior prom, who returned to the ball and danced till midnight; other times, seconds: a trigger, an envelope, a letter written on a Saturday morning — *Dear Mummy, I miss you. Hurry up.*

~

Back home, Kate wants to call Ray in Mexico to see if he's heard from Patti, but doesn't want to worry him unnecessarily. Patti might be on her way there. But what if she isn't?

In the end, she phones him. He's not home, so she leaves a message.

When he returns her call, it's evening. Her father is home and she feels awkward, as if she might give something away with her tone.

"Kate." Ray's voice is guarded. "What's wrong?" In the background, the strum of a Mexican guitar, women's laughter.

A small knot tangles in her stomach. "I'm calling about Patti," she says quickly.

Almost a year ago, when Ray came to Vancouver, she was feverish with joy and fear, hot and cold, as if she were experiencing a bout of malaria. She had promised herself she would be honest, tell him everything, beg forgiveness. Anything. She watched him descend the escalator, smiling, sandy hair tousled, blue jeans and black sweater, both wrists manacled in Tasco silver. A damp cold inched up her spine. By the time he'd crossed the baggage section, she had made herself believe that his casual slouch, his crooked smile, the lazy walk, were practised, artificial.

"Is she all right?" Ray asks now.

"I'm not sure." She describes the circumstances of Patti's disappearance, omits that Patti asked for her help to get away from Trevor. Patti could have meant anything, Kate reasons. Maybe she didn't like Trevor's friends, or his favourite TV programs; maybe she hated his drinking, or the way he kissed her; maybe she didn't want to be married any more.

Ray is silent for a moment. "She could have gone to the cabin," he says, finally. "But it's not fit to live in during winter."

You're her father, she wants to shout. *Go look for her!* She stares at the window, at her own reflection, nineteen years ago, in a motel room with Matt. Her father should have known. She would never have run away if he hadn't been too busy with Elaine. She waits, quiet, and when Ray still doesn't offer to come and look for Patti, says, "I could take a drive down to Pateros and have a look."

He sounds immensely relieved. "Great. Great. Call me as soon as you know either way. And I'll call you if she turns up here."

"Don't worry. She's probably all right," Kate says and hangs up.

Her father looks up from the book he's been reading. "Everything OK?"

"I'm worried about Patti."

"She's high-strung. All she needs is a bit of a break," Joe says. "She'll likely turn up tomorrow or the next day."

"I've got a bad feeling about it." Despite her reasoning, Kate doesn't really believe people vanish for no reason. Or do they? She recalls another Internet message:

> Subject: Missing on Purpose

Eleven years ago, I disappeared from Pittsburgh. I was hiding from an abusive drug-crazed husband. I went to live in Anchorage, Alaska, got a job and filed for divorce. I could tell no one where I was, without putting myself in danger. PLEASE BE AWARE THAT SOME PEOPLE WHO ARE LOOKING FOR A MISSING PERSON COULD BE THE REASON THAT PERSON IS MISSING.

Joe lays the book face down on the side table. "Look," he says, "sometimes things get overwhelming, and, well, running away seems like a good idea."

Escape, too, is a survival tactic. "Patti wouldn't have left the baby behind," she says. "I'm sure of it."

"You know, your mother — well, you couldn't have been more than a year old — she said, 'I can't stand it anymore. Let's just get in the car and drive. Get away from everything and everyone.' She really thought we could just drive off like that."

"What happened?" Kate asks.

"We went to stay with Rose for a couple of weeks. Iris was happy to come home." He smiles. "But maybe if she'd had a vehicle and a driver's licence, she'd have done what Patti's done."

"With or without me?" Kate says.

Her father shakes his head, the way one does with a person who has not understood.

I could use a little escape, Kate thinks, into a modern fairy tale, where the real Iris is a famous folksinger, who after years of fame, fortune and freedom, will come to claim Kate and they'll be on the cover of *People* magazine, and she'll get modelling jobs and movie offers and appear on *Oprah* and *The National*, and she'll move into Iris' fabulous house and meet a fabulous man and live a fabulously happy life ever after.

~

When Kate was three, she yearned for a different mother, perhaps one like Angie's, or even Angie herself, who was only eleven at the time. She dreamed of a mother who sang and laughed, who held her hand on pony rides; a mother on whose lap she could sit and be petted.

Instead, she had Iris, either the sullen, silent mother, or the distracted, wan one.

Some nights she closed her eyes and pretended that the woman in the next room was an impostor — that there'd been a mistake. When Iris disappeared, Kate was convinced she was responsible. Horrified and astonished by her own terrible power, she prayed for her mother's return. *Please, please, I'm sorry. I didn't mean it.*

~

Love, lovely, lover, lovestruck, lovesick, lovelorn, loveless.

Three-quarters of an hour into her drive south, when she reaches Pateros, Kate turns right, almost by instinct, as if her body needs to remember itself in a different context. Around the next corner, the cabin appears, exactly as she's seen it a thousand times in memory, its wood blackened with age and wear, its roof steep and witchy. She pulls up the dirt driveway and gets out of the car. The cabin is locked, but Ray always leaves the bathroom window unfastened for Patti.

"Patti?" she calls as she climbs the stairs. Her shoes leave thick prints in the dust. She walks the wraparound porch to the back, heels reverberating the wood's warm sound, like drums and heartbeats. She and Ray spent many hours here last summer, in the evenings. She would set the small table — madras tablecloth in brilliant ruddy tones, cloth napkins, two crystal wine glasses and bone-handled cutlery — and they would sit and eat, watching the stars slowly burn through the veneer of night. In the darkness, it was like meeting for the first time all over again. Both of them trying to disclose themselves and still remain concealed.

Kate told him about her weekly letters to her mother — a few sentences her father checked carefully for errors and untidiness. Once a week, a letter arrived from Iris. *Dear Kate, I am well. I have started playing guitar again. I miss you.* Her letters implied they'd soon be together again.

The August before Kate was to begin Grade 1, Iris wrote to say she was moving and would send an address as soon as she was settled. Kate waited, but no letter came. She continued to write her mother every Saturday, "so that Mummy will not feel so lonely," she told her father. In the envelope, she always included a drawing, her stick-people version of her and Joe inside the house, out in the yard, on the street, at school, her hand clutching his. She kept the letters in a box in her room, ready to send to Iris as soon as they heard from her.

Even after September, October and November passed, Kate didn't waver in her faith. On Christmas morning, when still no card or call had come, Kate was convinced that her mother would surprise them. She waited, nervous and excited, all day. That Christmas night, when her father kissed her good night and sent her up to bed, she refused to go.

"What's the matter?" he asked. "Haven't we had a lovely day?"

Kate nodded. She watched the Christmas lights twinkling in the black maw of the window.

"What then?" her father frowned.

"I just want to stay up a bit longer," she said. She went to the window and cupped her hands around her face, checking for headlights coming down the drive.

"What's this about?"

But Kate kept staring into the tunnel of night.

"It's ten thirty, way past your bedtime and mine, too." Joe touched her shoulder. "Let's go up and I'll tuck you in. Tomorrow we'll get up early and try out your new toboggan. What do you say?"

"Can we leave a light on?" she asked him.

"What for?"

"In case Mummy comes," she whispered.

Her father's face was a mixture of hurt, pity, sorrow. "Oh, Sweetheart," he murmured. He reached for her in an awkward, unfamiliar embrace. "Your mother is not coming," he said, his voice husky.

"But she said —"

"No." Firm.

"She's going to surprise us!" Kate cried, her chest a hollow, as if something had been vacuumed out.

"Kate, listen to me," Joe said, sofly. "It's been five months since your mother's last letter. She hasn't even sent her address."

"Maybe something happened to her," Kate said, hopeful.

"Nothing's happened to her. I would have been notified." He took her by the shoulders. "I know this is hard, but you've got to stop waiting for her."

In her chest the hollow solidified. She sat up very straight and hardened her face so that no expression showed. "She'll be back," she said to her father, her voice cold. "She'll be back, and she'll take me with her." She stood up then and took slow, robotic steps up to her room. She slid under the covers without undressing and started counting.

When her father knocked, she feigned asleep.

For months, she grieved in her dreams, cried out her mother's name in sleep, and Joe would awaken and go to sit by her bed, stroking her head until she hushed.

"And she never wrote?" Ray asked when Kate had finished.

She shook her head. They sat quiet for a while, hands entwined.

Ray told her about his father, a large, clumsy man who had been a mechanic since he was seventeen, who worked ten-hour days and called educated people "big shots." He had wanted Ray to become a doctor; he thought art was synonymous with loser. "My son, the doctor," Ray told her, mimicking his father in a bitter, sarcastic tone. "He'd introduce me that way to his friends, then laugh." He stared out into the warmth, and she held his hand tight.

"I started to paint him in my early teens," Ray said. "Small canvases. Ten-by-twelve. Black and white only." He paused. "I taped them to the walls of my room." Kate tried to imagine Ray's bedroom, walls filled with black sketches not of his father's features, but of his character. When he described them, they reminded her of Goya's *Disasters of War.* "I was trying to paint his disappointment," Ray told her.

One day, Ray came home from school and found all the canvases cut into one-inch strips. On his desk were brochures for various universities. He began to paint on hardboard, apple boxes, two-by-fours. His father sawed them into pieces, stacked them on a bonfire; left him pamphlets for the army, the Peace Corps, institutes of technology.

"What did your mother do?" Kate asked.

"What could she do? Nothing. He had sent for her, you

know, a mail-order bride from Greece. She said nothing and looked the other way." He was tense and wiry beside her.

Ray started painting on walls because it was the only thing his father couldn't destroy without damaging his own home.

"Ironically," Ray said, "when he retired, he took to making the most exquisite inlaid wooden tables. Hundreds of tiny pieces of wood — exotic grains and stains." He was quiet for a moment. "On a visit home years later," he said, "after my mother had died, and long after my father had stopped destroying my paintings, I went into the basement with an axe and hacked his precious tables into millions of pieces."

Kate didn't know what to say. It seemed shocking, that he had been able to hold that rage so carefully for so many years, that he had aimed it so precisely.

Now, as she walks around the porch, she sees fragments of Ray here: the tin cup on a windowsill, its coffee stains like tree rings; the old tire he sawed in two, then filled with earth and flowers; the oil drum in which he washed before coming inside; the half-finished patio he began to interlock near the end of summer. The remnants cluster into an empty ache.

She slides the bathroom window open, brushes dust off the windowsill, and crawls in. The air is stagnant, heavy. Ray didn't come back this spring. *Sounds serious.* Last year, Ray worked well into October before he came to Vancouver to see her.

In the front room, the walls are covered with murals. She recalls how anxious she was when she first arrived here, afraid of what she'd find. What if he turned out to be a mediocre artist? She had met too many people whose major accomplishments were talk. Would she love him nonetheless?

What attracted her to him was his remoteness. Ray, like her father, is enigmatic, unpredictable.

They met two years ago in Mexico where Kate and Angie had gone for a spur-of-the-moment December holiday. It was 1995, a year of fault lines splitting open — the Kobe earthquake that killed five thousand people, the assassination of Yitzhak Rabin; a year of extremists — the Oklahoma City bomber, Shoko Asahara of the Tokyo subway nerve-gas attack; the year of the discovery of the frozen body of a young Inca girl who, five hundred years before, had climbed the steep slope of Mount Ampato and offered herself as a human sacrifice.

Kate and Angie were walking around a small paving-stone square in Barra de Navidad, in front of a church when, through the open door, they noticed the large crucifix above the altar, and the Christ on it, whose arms hung, broken, at his side. It seemed fitting, Kate thought, that on his birthday, someone had released Christ's arms, had rescued him from an eternity of martyrdom. He didn't look quite so dead or imposing like this — more like a man who would, at any moment, pull out the nail from his feet and go on his way. Ray came up behind them — white linen shirt, stonewashed jeans, the laced thongs, olive skin, sandy shoulder-length hair, lanky body — there, in the midst of an albescent sky, a broken crucifix, a suggestion of miracles.

In Mexico that first week, his intensity was a darkness that could transform into a wondrous cocoon or a dungeon. She was seduced by the possibility of an immense love, of two people melding into one big cliché, like a TV ad for perfume. Of course, she didn't think this at the time; she was too busy imagining herself deliriously happy. Back in Vancouver, when he was phoning her every few days, the distance between them was an aphrodisiac.

Now, staring at the murals, she reexperiences the intense disappointment of her first viewing. Ray had told her he'd spent several winters studying Diego Rivera's murals at the Ministry of Education in Mexico City. He'd described his experiments with encaustic painting — in which pigment is mixed with hot wax and applied to the wall.

What she didn't expect to see was a photographic reproduction of some of Rivera's murals. Later, she identified them in a book: *The Embrace, Peasants, The Festival of the Corn Harvest, The Day of the Dead — City Fiesta*. The latter is the most impressive work, and it spreads across one solid wall of the cabin. In the background, a stage on which three large skeletons play guitars, their legs held together by pins, like marionettes.

Around and behind them on stage, two pyramids of skulls, crossbones and spectres. In the foreground, a crowd parties, some people seated, some standing, some eating from the roadside stands. Most interesting is that while this is a festival to honour the dead, the crowd in the mural is facing forward, away from the figures of death on stage. In the back row, Rivera's self-portrait stares at the viewer, something Ray also duplicated, replacing Rivera with himself.

In the original, the scene is urban, and Rivera treated his subjects satirically, showing the traditional festival turned into a raucous, drunken celebration. Ray's mural is set here — Kate recognizes the field in front of his house, the dirt road — and is devoid of cynicism. To one side, he has added a traditional rural scene: peasants praying at a gravesite, offering flowers, earthen pots of food, toys and gifts to their dead, burning candles and incense in their honour.

Now as then, she fails to see the significance of the reproduction of a work of art. Ray told her Rivera had left his native Mexico and gone to Europe for fourteen years, to study European art. In Spain, for example, Rivera sat in the Prado Museum and copied works by Goya, El Greco, Velázquez. "But this is *your* life, not a xerox of Rivera's," she said, and pointed to the mural. "What do these mean, here, in Pateros, in the U.S.?" She stares at it now, still puzzled by the fact that although Ray's technique is flawless, the mural is sterile.

She tiptoes past it, down the hall to Ray's bedroom — their bedroom. She sinks into the soft mattress, lies back against the pillow. But there is only a dank musty smell. Ray is in Mexico, making love to a new woman. He has not vanished.

Patti's been gone a week, she thinks, and no one cares. She could be hungry, in trouble. She could have had an accident. She could have been picked up on the highway by a madman. The papers are full of grisly stories; police stations are thick with Missing Persons files.

~

Motherless daughter, small happiness, Snow White, Cinderella, Beauty, Gretel, Rupunzel, Alice, the Little Match Girl, etc.

When she gets home, it's past noon, and both her father and Angie are packing the last of Elaine's things. In the centre of the living room, stacked boxes form a pyramid. For an absurd moment, Kate imagines this to be an art installation entitled PACKING. She stands, silent, in the doorway, but neither Joe nor Angie pays her any attention.

"Trevor's gone," Angie says, finally, as if to explain.

"Gone where?"

Angie shrugs. "He left a note. Said he'd be in touch when he gets to ... wherever he's going."

Kate rubs her forehead. *Please be aware that* .... "Has he gone after Patti?" she says, her voice sharp.

Joe looks up from the box he's been filling. "Trevor's gone to enrol in an electronics program," he says, calm. "That's all we know."

"And you believe that?" Kate says.

"Why shouldn't we believe that?" Angie sits at the edge of the couch, pulling the sleeves of her black ribbed turtleneck over her hands. "Trevor had planned to go to one of those technology schools. He would have gone out of high school if Patti hadn't gotten pregnant."

Kate stares at both of them in disbelief. "Who's going to look after the baby?" she asks.

"I'm looking after the baby," Angie says.

"Maybe you ought to talk to Ray," Kate says.

Angie rolls her eyes. "I don't think so," she says. "Ray's not exactly Superdad."

"You're not Supermom yourself," Kate says. She stomps upstairs and barricades herself in her room.

Matt calls unexpectedly, late afternoon, and asks Kate if she'd like to have a drink with him later. She hasn't seen him since the night of the funeral.

"I already have plans," she lies.

"A date?"

"Sort of."

"Another time, then," he says, and she can almost see him smile.

Stephen, 1984: the Golden Temple massacre, Indira Gandhi's assassination, the Union Carbide environmental disaster, the Ethiopian famine, the world's first donor-egg baby. She was halfway through her third year at the University of B.C. Stephen was her archaeology prof, and they'd been carrying on a flirtation for a few months — nothing serious, a lingering smile, an off-topic discussion during office hours.

They met for the first time off-campus on New Year's Eve. First Night, a Vancouver city party. Strings of white mini-lights hung in all the deciduous trees downtown, illuminating the skeletal frosty frames, transforming them into exotic sculptures with shimmering limbs, sparkling buds. Music blared from bandstands, wafted out of the open doors of nightclubs and restaurants. Everyone united, young families, pensioners, teenagers, girlfriends, buddies, lovers. Kate had been standing in line with a group of classmates in front of a nightclub when she saw Stephen. He was alone. They began to talk; her friends drifted away. At midnight, she and Stephen were in her apartment, beginning all over again.

The affair continued into her first year of graduate studies. In the fall of 1985, Stephen, armed with a research grant and a sabbatical, asked her to join him in field research at the ancient Mayan city of Nakbe, in northern Guatemala. She remembers enormous temples abandoned almost two thousand years before by a vibrant, advanced culture that literally vanished, leaving secrets buried under a thick mantle of tropical rainforest, a stone tool, half carved, flakes all around it, as if someone had simply put it down mid-work, and walked away; a tiny ceramic head. Burials fixed in time. They slept under a sky dense with stars; rose in the morning to heat, humidity, ticks, snake bites.

A year later, Stephen published a paper they had co-written, and he did not give her credit. She was furious, humiliated, but Stephen managed to convince her that she had been fortunate to have been on-site, that her career benefited, that they would go on to co-author other things, that they would get married.

Three years later when he still hadn't left his wife, she gave him an ultimatum on November 24th, the anniversary of Iris' leaving. That New Year's Eve, she sat alone in her apartment, thinking about the affair, about "How to Boil a Frog," a science experiment from high school. If you put a frog in boiling hot water, it'll jump out to save itself. However, if you put the frog in cool water, then slowly heat it, it will become conditioned to the temperature and not jump out, even when the water is hot enough to boil it.

She must have been standing, staring into space, because her father now says, "That was Matt," then waits, as if he expects an explanation.

"Ah-huh," she says, and walks past him, up the stairs.

Earlier, Joe helped her carry the hardboard wardrobe upstairs to her room. It's lined with cedar shakes and filled almost entirely with clothes that Kate wants to examine for clues about her mother — Iris' tastes and preferences in colours, shapes. She takes out each item and holds it against her. There are slim pants, pedal-pushers, skirts, dresses and fitted sweaters in vibrant lime greens, magentas, oranges. No pastels, no flowery patterns; only bold lines and geometric designs. She tries them on, surprised by how well everything fits. Then, at the bottom of the box, under the last sweater, she finds the taffeta skirt.

Immediately she recognizes the pattern — a harlequin geometry of diamonds; the colours — greens, purples, reds against black background; the shape — a full circle that comes down to mid-calf. She can see Iris wearing it over several crinolines one sunny day out on the porch. Kate must have been three or four, watching Iris through the screen door. She had been awakened by loud rock 'n' roll music and had gone to find her mother.

TAFFETA SKIRT: HARDBOARD WARDROBE [8]

Iris is jiving with a man Kate doesn't know, her feet skipping up and down the porch, the two of them in perfect synch, straight out of an Arthur Murray dance competition. Every few moves, he twists his arm, and round she goes, taffeta skirt flaring, rustling like a spring creek. Kate watches her, riveted, until the song ends and a new, slow one begins. The man's arm circles Iris' waist and pulls her close, so that the skirt flutes like fancy pie crust, exposes crinolines underneath. Iris leans her head back and laughs, her arms reaching around his neck.

"Mummy," Kate calls out, and begins to cry.

They spring apart and Iris comes toward Kate, her face a dark frown. "Why aren't you in your room?" she says. "I told you to stay in your room!"

Kate runs, frightened, down the hall. The screen door slams and her mother hurries after her, holds her, says she's sorry, while the man watches them from where he stands just inside the door.

She reaches into the wardrobe and holds the skirt against her face, but smells only cedar. She sheds her jeans, zips on the skirt. It fits perfectly, and when she looks in the mirror, she sees Iris. She peels off her sweatshirt and puts on one of Iris' black fitted sweaters, the one with three-quarter-length sleeves and a dramatic V neckline that begins at the shoulders. Then she takes the jet choker out of the jewellery box and fastens it round her neck. She'll wear it tonight. Maybe do a little dancing herself. She twirls twice and watches the skirt rise and wave in a Chinese ribbon dance.

She remembers a photo of Iris in her father's album: she's wearing the skirt and leaning against a doorway, staring into the distance, one hand in her pocket, the other holding a cigarette whose smoke wafts upwards. She strikes the same pose, minus the cigarette, and when she slips her hand in the hidden side pocket of the skirt, she touches a piece of cardboard. She pulls it out and stares at the photo of the young man in her memory. WAVY BLACK

HAIR, LIGHT EYES, MICK JAGGER LIPS, WHITE SHIRT UNBUTTONED AT THE NECK. He is so young and beautiful, she can almost forgive her mother, can almost fall in love with him herself. She wonders what his name is and why Iris left his photo behind.

She goes looking for her father who, with Angie, is packing and moving things downstairs. "Dad?" she calls.

Her father comes out into the hall and freezes when he sees her on the landing.

"I ... found it in the trunk," she says. She's in the middle of a *déjà-vu* — a hallucination, perhaps, because in this memory she's wearing the taffeta skirt and walking down the stairs toward her father, who takes her hand and guides her out onto the porch where they dance.

"I don't think you should wear that," he says, half whispering.

Angie steps out into the hall. "What's the matter?" she says, and that breaks whatever spell has fallen on them.

Kate walks past both of them and goes into the kitchen to pour herself a drink.

Her father follows her in. "Isn't it a bit early?" he says.

She takes the photo out of her pocket and puts it on the counter in front of him. "Who's that?"

He picks it up, looks at it, and puts it back down. "I don't know." He pauses. "Where'd you find it?"

"Is that the guy she went off with?"

"I said I don't know who it is," he says, his words clipped.

His face is an iron shield, like that of a masked friend. They remain fixed, staring at each other. Abruptly, he turns his back. She gulps her drink, goes upstairs and gets her purse. Then she drives, aimless, up the highway.

As she approaches the diner, she sees the sinister silhouettes of heavy machinery: the graders — large, prehistoric monsters with buckets half raised to some mythical god; the crane's gigantic hook like a hangman's noose. She wonders what secrets are buried there, what surprises could emerge if someone were to sift through the soil — miners, loggers, ditch-walkers, ranchers, bones, artifacts — everyone, everything touching.

The sky is a dim fisherman's net. A twilight trap.

She drives through town, the one short street. Everything's closed. Everyone's gone. Absence is a blue perfume, an oboe melody in the desert; absence has the texture of polished chrome, the taste of absinthe on the tongue.

In Winthrop, she finds an Internet café and checks her e-mail again. She punches in "Missing Persons" and scrolls through pages of news stories and message boards until she finds one called *Missing Mothers*.

Subject: Missing mother 20 years ago

I have been looking for my beloved mother
for the past 13 years. She left me when I was
3 years old. Because my father was a salesman,
and he was travelling at the time, she called

my grandparents to come and get me. Then, she dropped me with my babysitter and just vanished. Her name was Julia Howard. Any information would be greatly appreciated.

Subject: Missing mother's right to privacy?

It bothers me when someone tells me that my missing mother has the "right to privacy," as if that's more important than the pain I'm going through. Please come back. No questions answered.

Subject: Holidays make the loss feel worse

Every holiday, I begin anticipating the return of my missing mother. Somehow, I expect that she is going to show up at the door. It hasn't happened yet, and probably won't this year either, but I'm still hoping.

Subject: Missing Mother Artist

: Missing/Mother
: Dorothy Forsight
: Age: 33
: 5' 6" tall, thin
: Blue eyes
: Mole on left cheek, below eye
: Artist – usually carried sketch book with her
: Missing since March 1995

: Please contact family with information
: I LOVE YOU

Subject: Missing Mother since 1970

I am looking for my mother who hung out with
Purple Pumpkins, a rock band from Denver,
Colorado. She is the oldest of 3 daughters and
she left behind my sister and me. Although I
don't have any idea why she disappeared, I don't
hate or resent her. I just want to find her and
give her a chance to pick up where she left off.

Subject: My Mom went missing 25 years ago

Betty Calvert is about 60 years old now. She
was born in Port Isaac, Cornwall, and came to
Canada as a child. We were living in Kingston,
Ontario, when she went missing. She had called
us from Toronto where she was visiting a friend,
to say that her car had broken down. She was
going to take the train home. We never saw her
again. I still love her madly and miss her terribly.
I was never ever angry at her for going.

Kate sits and stares at the messages, astounded by their
tone. Such yearning, such misdirected love. *Beloved …
Please come back … I love you … I want to give her a chance
to pick up where she left off … I still love her madly and miss
her terribly.* A missing mother doesn't talk back, doesn't

betray you, doesn't complain, criticize or attack you. A missing mother cannot abandon you. Kate types two messages:

> **Subject: Newborn needs missing mother**
>
> I am a newborn, searching for my mother, Patti Konstantin. She is 17, rides a motorcycle and is incredibly irresponsible. Come home now, Mother. We haven't even bonded.

> **Subject: To A Selfish Missing Mother**
>
> I am looking for my inconsiderate, selfish mother, Iris Mason (neé Hinton), who left a husband and small girl (me, 4 years old) 29 years ago, to run off with one of her lovers. If you're reading this, Mother, I just want you to know that no matter how romantic your life sounds in the retelling, I don't love you madly, and I'm still furious at you for leaving.

She does not include her e-mail address.

When she arrives at The Palace, it's almost ten o'clock, and the tavern is loud with weekend tourists and locals, mostly in jeans, T-shirts and fleece vests in cutesy arctic patterns — dancing polar bears, igloos and seals. She feels overdressed in the taffeta skirt and clingy top. She orders a drink and stands against a post, watching the band.

The avalanche of sound frees her to think. Takes her back to that Mexican honeymoon, Christmas lights draped on the pyramid palapa roof, white tablecloths, plastic chairs, the ocean thundering beside them. Ray. Is he standing now against the coral wall of a Mexican tavern, leaned into a young woman? *Sounds serious.* They've been divorced only four months.

The band breaks, and the sax player walks toward her. She realizes she has been staring at him for the past three songs, not seeing his soft black eyes.

"You don't look from around here," he says. "Where do you call home?"

Home. Direction: Vancouver, Twisp, Kitimat, Pateros. Bearing: Rose, Dad, Iris, Ray — cities and people confused. Like a tribe returning after a catastrophe to find rubble, water, the landscape so altered it's impossible to recognize the place that exists so vivid in memory.

She forces herself to smile, and he signals a round, nods her toward the band booth where the drummer paradiddles on the edge of the table and the bass player soundlessly fingers his bass. *Each to his own distraction.* She drinks two more scotches, neat, in the next twenty minutes, while the sax player chitchats, until, finally, he hops up on stage. Kate turns her head to signal the waitress for another drink, and there, in the mirror behind the bar, is Iris. She sucks in her breath and looks away.

The sax player is an excellent musician; the notes dynamic, expressive. If she closes her eyes, she can hear a heart beating, nothing else; on her lids, a giant scrim of a palpitating heart. Gradually, everyone stops talking so that the sax melody gains in clarity and volume, its seductive wail reaching everyone in the room. She watches, aware that music erases the physical lines of the flesh and it's possible to be aroused by emotions expressed through the instrument, to desire the performer whose music moves her, false intimacy, inarticulate and raw. The blues notes echo from somewhere deep inside him, echo deep within her, so that before she knows it, she's following him into a small motel room. She is reduced to physical properties: protein chains, cells, amino acids, nucleosides, DNA, RNA ... lips, breasts, nipples, thighs ... body open, heart valves shut. A desertion, while her mind returns to Mexico.

"I have never loved you," she told Ray that day at the Vancouver airport. She'd been practising the phrase for weeks, trying to make herself believe it. To repress something you have to forget it, be unaware that it existed before you forgot it, be unaware that you have forgotten it, and be unaware that you have forgotten that you have forgotten it. Her memory was intact. Sometimes, she thinks, the past lies in the fault line of our brain, tethered between knowing and not knowing, between desire and need.

In the morning, her head feels packed with plaster of Paris. The sax player is still asleep beside her, black hair coiled on the pillow, odd strands caught in his eyelashes, his face childlike. She makes herself breathe, slow and even. This isn't the last day of a cruise or an anonymous city she can disappear into. She gets up, dresses and escapes into the morning frost.

Once she's back in her car, she mouths silent prayers and makes deals with God, if only her father will not hear about this one. She begins to invent a story to tell him .... Perhaps Angie will cover for her. *Grow up. It doesn't matter what he thinks.* She sticks in her CD of Leonard Cohen hits and listens to his gravelly voice: "Everybody knows that the naked man and woman / are just a shining artifact of the past .... "

Three miles down the road, she turns a corner and finds eight or nine cars parked on the shoulder, her father's and Matt's among them. People swarm on both sides of the highway. She parks too, then hurries toward Matt.

"Patti's motorcycle's been found in the ravine," he says.

"Where's Patti?" she asks, her heart pounding.

"It's just the bike," Matt says. "Dumped, by the looks of it." He points. "Joe's taken a search party to the other side."

A search *party*. Beach party. House party. She imagines laughter, music, ice smashing in glasses.

They've been searching for several hours already, awaiting the two leashed German shepherds and their handlers from Wenatchee. As soon as they arrive, her father gives the handlers Patti's sweater, which the dogs sniff before scrambling into the ravine, tugging at their leashes. Matt and another police officer veer in different directions, cell phones out, whistles blowing, flagging down cars, herding the searchers to the right, to the left, over that mound, past those trees, as if they were waves of locusts over the landscape. Angie stands to one side, the baby in her arms. It all feels somewhat surreal, as if Kate has stepped into a movie set, and someone will at any moment yell, "Cut!" She presses forward, toward Angie, aware of the swish of her skirt, thinking, *gross stress*, thinking, *anticipatory, impact, recoil, post-traumatic*.

Then, the dogs begin to bark and yelp.

"Over here! Bring the shovels!" one of the handlers yells.

The dogs dig, furious paws scraping up dirt, noses into the ground, tails flapping and twirling. Two volunteers bring shovels and begin to dig gingerly. *Anticipatory. Anticipatory.* Patti's suitcase is the first thing uncovered. Kate feels a horrible capsizing sensation. Angie stands across from her, staring into the shallow grave, her face white, her eyes unblinking. Kate feels disoriented, watching Patti emerge one bit at a time — a hand, an arm, a shoulder — a burial in reverse, a resurrection, only it isn't like TV where the body, the features, are perfectly preserved. This Patti is a bluish white, bloated and decomposed, maggots squirming in her eyes and nose and mouth. The air is foul with putrid flesh. Kate sees the baby then, facing the grave in Angie's arms, and she yanks her from Angie and shields her from the terrible sight of her mother's body.

Isolations

August 4, 1997 / *Pacific Princess*

THE IK

"Imagine for a moment what would happen to our family and social structures if we suddenly experienced an environmental catastrophe that had us living in permanent hunger, with many among us starving to death.

"Presumably we would band together, strengthen our family ties, fiercely protect our young and help our brothers and sisters.

"Now imagine these 'natural' responses abandoned in favour of self-preservation. Imagine that the concept of sharing no longer exists, so that you could be well-fed while your sibling or parent or child starves beside you.

"Impossible? No. An extraordinary adaptation in the face of extinction. I could be describing an apocalyptic film instead of a very real people from northern Uganda, called the Ik.

"Historically the Ik were nomadic and hunted in and around the Kidepo Valley, up into the Sudan and down into Kenya, in a loose triangle that disregarded political boundaries. Over a period of thirty to forty years, the Ik's cycle was disrupted — partly by environmental conditions such as long periods of drought, partly by a tightening of national borders. As a result, they experienced permanent hunger and frequent starvation.

"Instead of drawing together and helping each other, the Ik slowly fragmented all social systems and began to pursue most activities by themselves. They searched for food and water alone, survival being more likely if they didn't share their findings. If you were there, you might see a robust young man sitting beside his starving sister or mother or wife. He might be eating whatever he found that day while his starving relative looks on. He would not offer to share his food and she, the sister or mother or wife, would not expect him to.

"We've seen sci-fi movies about this sort of thing: a nuclear holocaust, perhaps, the possibility of global destruction. Suddenly everyone is fending for himself, hoarding, without a thought of sharing. It's as if a survival mechanism has kicked in and turned people into psychopaths, without feelings, without conscience. No, we don't like to think that we could actually do this, do we? But how do we know we wouldn't if the conditions were bad enough?

"In the Ik's case, their conditions became so extreme that by the 1960s, they considered deprivation to be the norm, and any abundance — either in crops or government aid — as the exception, unpredictable and not to be relied on. Like the Kaiadilt, they thought the natural world was not to blame; rather, they saw themselves as inadequate.

"Another extraordinary thing about the Ik is that they dismissed all that we consider 'natural,' — things like relationships, the mother-child bond, nurturing. For example, men and women did marry, but their union had nothing to do with love and companionship. Instead, it had to do with need. Each needed someone to help build a shelter, which would make survival more likely. In the Ik language, the word for 'love' is the same as for 'want' or 'need.'

"When a woman became pregnant, her first reaction was one of anger, because her own survival was now compromised. If the child was born, she breast-fed him for three years. After that, she stopped nourishing him and, although he could stay within the compound, he was no longer allowed to sleep in the house — he had to provide his own shelter. To prepare him for this, the mother subjected the child to deliberate abuse beginning from age two — to teach the child that he could rely on no one, not even her. Unthinkable? Certainly by our standards. How did the child manage?

"Well, at the age of three, the child joined a gang of children aged three to eight, and hunted with them, mainly as a protection against predators. These predators included adult Iks who had introduced a new concept, *goodness,* into the language, for their own survival. Any adult who could take food away from a child was a *good* adult. The gangs roamed the gullies and whoever found food devoured it at once. The children neither fought over nor shared food. At about eight, the child was thrown out of this gang and joined a senior gang. When he reached twelve, he was considered an adult and expected to hunt alone. Only the fastest and strongest children survived."

GARNET RING: MIXED FRUIT DROP TIN [16]

When Iris discovered she was pregnant, eight months after leaving home, her first reaction was anger. Most of it was directed at Joe, who, she believed, should not have let this happen. This was before Iris learned to be responsible for her body.

Joe's reaction to her pregnancy was to offer her a garnet ring and a proposal, which she accepted, partly because she was disillusioned with her nonexistent singing career, partly because she believed herself in love with him. She packed her belongings and boarded a bus to Wenatchee, where Joe waited to take her home to Twisp.

"My life is over," she wrote to Elaine a month later, the letter sent to one of Elaine's friends.

"Please, Daddy, let me come home," she wrote to her father, who, after reading the letter, folded it and tore it into sixteen fragments, which he then flushed down the toilet. He did not want a sullen, withdrawn teenager to come home and quarrel with her mother. He did not want to fight about her taste in clothes, her hairstyle, her grades, her curfew, her every move. He did not want a pregnant teenager to embarrass him. He did not want a daughter he could not control.

Kate imagines Iris as an Ik woman, solitary, isolated from family, friends, country. But what if Iris was simply a self-obsessed teenager who made a series of bad choices and didn't want to take responsibility for them? In the Ik language, the word for "love" is the same as the word for "want" and "need." What if Kate had had Matt's baby when she was fifteen? Would she have cared for it? Or would she have yearned to be like other teenagers, going to parties, dating, discovering the world for herself? What if Iris' lovers were not a way to abate loneliness, but a way to force Joe to let her go? Kate has always known about her mother's lovers — Angie armed her before she was ten, afraid Kate might be called a bastard, be lured into fist fights, made to defend her mother.

When she became an adolescent, Kate's mother-yearning metamorphosed into shame. How could she be expected to know what to say? What to do? What to be? How could she model herself after a mother, who, in the town's eyes, had disgraced herself, a mother who had abandoned her? Terrified that the other girls would think her different, abnormal, she reinvented herself: she was a woman who needed no one. She was on the honour roll.

She won lead roles in school productions. She was captain of the girls' basketball team, the class treasurer, the one to whom others went for comfort. She was strong, in control. *She* was a role model. She was unleavable.

In 1978, however, the night Joe brought Elaine home for the first time, Kate took her father's keys, got in his car and drove it eighty miles an hour, until one of the wheels caught on the gravel shoulder and flipped the car into a ditch. Kate sat, stunned, nothing broken except her heart. When Joe sent her to summer camp later that year, she swam halfway across the lake, even though she knew she was not a strong swimmer, and almost drowned. And finally, when Joe announced that he and Elaine had married, Kate tried to elope with Matt.

In Vancouver, being parentless gave her special status, access to an exclusive clique of sullen, black-clad, spiky-haired teenagers for whom alcohol and cigarettes were fashion accessories, for whom rebellion was a virtue. There were no *virgins,* no *girls* in this lot, there were only *women.*

The confusion: there hasn't been a suspicious death in Twisp for as long as anyone can remember. The air is a buzz of morbid excitement, anticipation, dread. People crane to see Patti's body, flinch, stare, avert their eyes. There is the restless shuffle of feet, the hum of voices, speculating. But this is not like TV, where the killer is a psychopath living in an inner city apartment with his macabre fantasies. *I've got to get away from here ... from*

Trevor …. Patti's voice stabs a huge guilt-hole in Kate's brain. The most likely killer, it seems obvious to Kate, is Trevor, and he's the kid-next-door, anybody's son. Why didn't she listen? Why didn't she do something?

"Stop, everyone!" Joe says abruptly, in the middle of the digging.

Everyone freezes, turns to him, surprised.

He waves his hands and walks toward them, shooing everyone back a few feet, as if they were pigeons in a public park. "We must establish a safe zone," he says.

They've probably already contaminated all the evidence, Kate thinks. Last year at the Maryland dig, when they inadvertently uncovered recent human remains, Kate worked closely with a forensic anthropologist brought in to determine the time and cause of death, to give a name, a life, to the remnants of the young woman who, they later discovered, had been murdered by a jealous boyfriend. The Locard Exchange Principle: *Every contact leaves a trace.* Fingerprints on the body's surface, dead skin cells sloughed onto clothing, hair, saliva, semen — the body, a veritable pool of evidence.

Here in Twisp, right now, her father and Matt are suddenly concentrating on protocol, this being one they aren't familiar with. Matt has taken yellow barrier tape out of his trunk and is tying it to shrubs and trees in a free-form square around the grave. Meanwhile, he's trampling everything as he goes. He *should* be taking extreme caution not to disturb anything nearby. Often, the most important clues come from the surrounding area — clues that might indicate who buried Patti, whether she was killed here or elsewhere. Even the time of death can be determined by examining the colonies of insects in the immediate vicinity. But the ground has already been trampled by the enthusiastic volunteers and now, Joe and Matt are trying to compensate with officiousness.

Kate focuses on the baby in her arms, thinking, *This child will never meet her mother. There'll be no search, no hope for a reunion.* She stares at the ground, at Patti's waxen hand. Should she have tried harder, both with Patti and with Ray? She hugs the baby to her chest, as if it were a crucifix. But she is neither religious nor superstitious. She looks into the grave, at her father's back, at Angie's flushed cheeks.

In the air, an outbreak of fear and revulsion and relief. The volunteers have rearranged themselves into pairs, trios and clusters. They speak in hushed tones, as if guarding secrets from the dead, cigarettes clinging to their lips or between their dusty fingers.

"We're all responsible for Patti's death," Kate says, and Joe and Matt turn, frowning in unison at her, as if she were a singing drunk stumbling up the aisle of a wedding in progress. Then Joe narrows his eyes into a familiar disapproving look.

"We could have prevented this," she continues, her voice rising in pitch in direct proportion to her involuntary regression into childhood.

"Kate." Joe's voice is firm, authoritative. "We have this under control."

Kate looks from him to Matt, who avoids her eyes. *Patti's dead*, she thinks, *and nobody cares*. "What about Ray?" she says, loud. "Ray ought to know."

"I'll call Ray as soon as things are settled here," Joe says. "There's protocol. We can't make mistakes. It's crucial to the investigation."

"What are you talking about?" she says, her guilt transformed into righteous fury. "There's nothing to investigate. Pick up Trevor. End of story."

In two quick strides, Joe is beside her, his fingers digging into her upper arm, his eyes tight and small. "Butt out, Kate," he says quietly. "There will be no vigilante action here. We'll make an arrest when we have concrete evidence."

Kate looks around, confused. The crowd shuffles; someone asks Joe if he should call for backup. The baby begins to fret in Kate's arms and Angie claims her. Kate feels everyone falling away from her. And then she sees herself in the taffeta skirt and clingy top, last night's date, and she turns and runs to her car.

All the way home, she marvels at how people's lives continue, untouched by death. Behind The Yellow Jacket shop windows, a salesclerk punches numbers on an old-fashioned till, her hand orchestrating the tourists' march through the antiques; two teenagers drink coffee in the window booth of The Branding Iron, cigarettes held high, faces bored; a young man leans against the glass of a phone booth, lips smiling into the mouthpiece; a middle-aged couple walk by, hand in hand; a mother and daughter argue on the porch of a small house, both with hands on hips, like children spiting each other; cars wind up and down Main Street.

Kate feels an overwhelming sense of emptiness. All around her these strangers appear purposeful, connected. She imagines herself settling here, nodding to people on the street, living on a ranch by the river, square dancing on Saturday nights. She knows, of course, this is a sentimental version of small-town life, a sentimental version of any life.

If she were in the city, she could duck into a bar and have a drink. Here, she fishes through her purse for her bottle of diazepam, swallows a pill. "You're addicted to them," Rose says, which is probably true. But it's a small price to pay for inner peace.

Time travel. Her car heads for Matt's house. She's not sure what she's going to do when she gets there, but as she approaches, she sees a woman, Barbara, she assumes, out in the yard pruning hedges, and two young boys playing on the step by the door. She cringes, her neck and ears burning, but can't turn back. She wonders if Barbara knows who she is, if Matt has told his wife about her. As she approaches, Barbara looks up, lifts her left arm to shield her eyes from the sun and stares at her as she drives past.

She continues up the highway, toward the coast, which seems almost another galaxy at the moment. She thinks of Rose in her Gastown office with its floor-to-ceiling windows facing the harbour; Rose arcing in her black leather recliner, eyes gazing at the North Shore mountains, phone cradled between ear and shoulder as she makes deals with concert promoters and band leaders. She thinks of her own apartment, of all her possessions piled in the centre of the living room, still unpacked, as they have been for the past six weeks.

For a moment, she imagines that room as an anthropological dig a thousand years in the future. HIDE-A-BED, A BUNDLE OF CLEAN CLOTHES ON HANGERS, IKEA COFFEE TABLE, A BOX OF UNMATCHED PINK DEPRESSION GLASS AND A CUTLERY TRAY HEAPED WITH KITCHEN UTENSILS AND CHOPSTICKS, A GLASS TABLETOP — SUPPORT LEGS MASKING-TAPED TOGETHER, TWO DISASSEMBLED MAPLE BOOKCASES, FOUR GARBAGE BAGS JAMMED WITH ASSORTED TOWELS, BEDDING, KITCHEN CLOTHS, CLEANING FLUIDS, TOILETTE ARTICLES, COSMETICS, PHONE BOOKS, TWO OLD BENTWOOD CHAIRS WITH RATTAN SEATS, THREE BOXES OF BOOKS AND NOTES, A LAPTOP COMPUTER, A STARBUCKS' CAPPUCCINO MACHINE AND TWO POUNDS OF ESPRESSO. But those items don't tell her story; all the important parts are missing. *It's not how much you lose, but who.* Her anthology of extinctions grows daily. If she were home right now, she'd sort through everything, put her life into perspective. If she were home right now, Joe, Elaine, Patti,

Angie would be distant names. Instead, she has stepped into the eye of their stormy lives and, for a moment, she understands Iris' instinct to flee, no forwarding address, new life.

She steps on the gas and suddenly she's climbing up to Washington Pass and there's nowhere to turn around. The sky darkens like a partial eclipse created by stratus clouds and sheer mountain peaks. The temperature drops quickly, fat flakes splatter against the windshield and the forest is dusted with snow. She turns up the heat and curses the taffeta skirt. At the top of the pass, she's able to swerve right into a lookout where she turns the car and drives back down into the valley.

At the house, she phones Ray. "You must come immediately," she says, when he finally answers, his voice husky with sleep and distance.

"Where's Patti?" he asks, alarmed.

She's incapable of forming the words, wishing she could spare him this.

"Is she all right?" he says, hopeful.

"No." She begins to weep.

"Kate," he says, firm. "What happened?"

"I don't know what happened," she says, "but she's dead."

After she hangs up, she stands in front of the kitchen window and cries, but it's not for Patti, or Ray, or anyone or anything specific. Bursts of memory surface and she's here at two, four, eight, thirteen ... she is always here, always alone, staring out the window, waiting.

When her eyes dry, she climbs the stairs to her room — Elaine's room — and stares at the unfinished quilt. She lays out all the pieces and begins to baste them together, the needle digging into her index finger. Don't worry about the things you can't change, she tells herself, and change the things you can.

I can find Iris. If I can reconstruct an extinct culture, I can certainly find my cringing, cowardly, runaway mother.

She picks up the next quilt piece, a green square, and frowns. The piece is cut from one of the diamonds in the taffeta skirt. When she holds it against her, it disappears into the skirt. She picks up a new square, from another of Iris' skirts, and another and another. She opens the wardrobe and rearranges Iris' clothes, hangs them so she can see them all at once. Iris must have made her own clothes, left remnants that Elaine found. *I haven't paid enough attention.* She picks up piece after piece, trying to decipher the colours, patterns, shapes of memories, iden-tities. The taffeta skirt rustles with her every movement, and she stares at the brilliant diamonds, thinking, *we are a collection of stories ordered into narrative.*

"Mother," she says out loud.

But the fragments yield nothing.

When she has stitched the top of the quilt, she goes downstairs and makes herself a sandwich. She phones Rose and tells her about Patti, then she tries her dad at the station. The receptionist tells her that forensic scientists — pathologist, anthropologist, entomologist — have flown up from Seattle. Joe has gone with them to the trailer to take samples, dust furniture for prints and god knows what else. She wonders if Trevor is already in custody, if Angie is covering for him.

~

In the dream, two sets of trousered legs drag a folded rug along the ground through thick shrub. They are struggling with its weight, breathing heavily, grunting. Now and then they stop, and, where the rug comes slightly unfurled, she can see the top of a head, the heel of a foot — marble white and translucent. Twigs snap back, break; leaves cling to the fibres of the rug; a comet of dust follows the footsteps, clings to low branches and wildflowers.

Then a booted foot stomps a shovel into the ground, over and over again, while beside it, a second set of feet — in dirty Adidas — scuffs the earth. And here the dream expands, reveals another set of feet and another, then faces, until all the residents of Twisp are present, each taking a turn at the shovel. Beside the deepening hole, Patti lies in the unfurled blanket.

~

Kate leaves early the next morning, although it is only ninety-two miles to the Wenatchee airport. Last night when Ray called to say he'd be arriving at noon today, she told him she'd pick him up. Patti's death has transported them to a previous past, given her one more chance.

She drives an hour past Pateros, the Columbia River roaring beside her. At the Wenatchee airport, her stomach is clenched and she's run out of antacid tablets. She paces, trying to decide what she should say first. What will she do if he collapses against her in tears? She is uncomfortable with emotional displays, prefers her friends to appear solid. Paradoxically, she also longs for them to burst into spectacular sentimental carnivals.

When she sees him, finally, he walks toward her in jeans, a short-sleeved denim shirt, silver-and-stone pendants, chokers, bracelets, his fingers weighed down with massive rings in the shape of wild animals. Instead of boots, he wears Nike runners and white sports socks. He walks slowly, with the slight rocking movement chameleons make, with their long thin legs and short necks, their crests, horns and spines changing colour in response to light, temperature, fear. She marvels at his ability to surprise her, to both attract and repel her.

When he is in front of her, sombre and composed, she presses herself into his arms. He holds her, arms stiff and awkward.

"I've booked you a room at the Idle-a-While," she says, embarrassed. "It's not fancy —"

"Fine," he says and runs a hand through his hair.

They walk out to the parking lot and he slides his carry-on across the back seat.

On the drive, Ray sits silent, staring out the window, his head turned away from her.

"I'm really sorry about Patti," she says, finally.

He turns to her. "I should have come when she had the baby," he says and shakes his head.

She's not sure what he knows about Trevor, what her father might have told him. "When did you see her last?" she asks.

"Last summer. With you." He doesn't look at her.

Would things be different if she and Ray were still together? A week before Kate left last summer, Patti had returned to Twisp, the result of an argument that began after supper one day, in mid-August, when Kate offered to drive Patti to Wenatchee to buy her new school clothes and supplies. Patti had been flipping through *Vogue, Seventeen, Mirabella* and *People* magazines, moping in a hammock on the porch. She was about to go into Grade 11, and Kate thought a shopping trip might cheer her up.

Patti said, "I don't want to go back to school."

Ray and Kate had looked at each other, surprised. Patti hadn't said anything to this effect before. "You've got to finish high school," Kate said.

"I want to come and live with you in Mexico, Daddy," Patti said, ignoring Kate.

Ray looked away. They hadn't yet discussed whether they'd move to Mexico or Twisp, or Vancouver, whether they'd continue to live in separate countries and come together on holidays, whether this marriage would go on.

"You'll finish school and then we'll talk about it," Ray said.

"No, I fucking won't!" Patti slapped her hand on the table.

"You watch your mouth!"

"I'll fucking well say what I like!"

Kate walked out onto the porch trying to block out the sound of her and Joe's voices all those years ago. Finally Ray emerged with Patti's suitcases and hurled them into the jump seat of his pickup. Kate started to say something, but Ray silenced her with a look. Patti came out carrying a wooden apple box overflowing with CDs, magazines, sandals and motorcycle parts. She slammed the box in the back, next to the motorcycle Ray had already secured, then got in the front passenger seat, crossed her arms and stared straight ahead. Ray mumbled, "I'm taking her back to Twisp. See you in an hour or so."

Patti and Ray had had several blow-ups in the previous weeks and had made it clear Kate's opinion was unwelcome. Kate could see their shouting wasn't going to help much; Ray was going to get his way no matter what.

Patti returned to board with Angie and Trevor, got pregnant and is now dead, Kate thinks. It doesn't seem possible that it has all happened in a year.

Beside her, Ray shifts and crosses his right leg over his left. "I should have taken her with me to Mexico," he says. "If she'd been with me, this wouldn't have happened."

"It's no good wondering," Kate says.

"Anything would have been better than this." He stares out the window, leaves Kate alone, empty.

At Pateros, she asks if he wants to stop at the cabin, but he shakes his head.

Near Twisp, she wonders where she should take him: the motel? her father's house? Precht's Methow Valley Chapel?

"Turn here," Ray says, before she can ask. "I want to pick up my truck."

She lets him out in front of a beat-up garage and drives away, thinking of all the things they haven't said.

Joe is asleep in the living room, his uniformed body folded into a recliner, his face slack. Kate tiptoes past him, toward the stairs, but he hears her and calls out.

"I dropped Ray off," she says. "He's probably gone to the chapel."

He nods and stretches. "I better get down there."

"Any news?" she asks.

"Some," he says and gets up. "Patti's body was moved. Twice." The entomologist found evidence of insects on her body that were not indigenous to the grave site. Kate knows that insects begin to take flesh off a body minutes after death; that they start in the wound sites and natural orifices — eyes, nostrils, mouth; that in twenty-four hours they can turn a head into a skull; that depending on the site and temperature, different colonies of insects arrive.

In Patti's case, some of the pupa casings found in the grave came from another location.

"Quite likely from the back of the trailer," Joe says, "because the bathroom rug she was wrapped in contained traces of landfill the construction crews had dumped there." He pauses. "We found insects that matched the pupa casings found inside the trailer, too."

"So she was killed in the trailer and moved twice," she says.

"Not unusual in a homicide," Joe says. "The murderer could have been surprised and had to hide the body quickly."

"It must have been Trevor," she says.

"Nothing specific enough yet," Joe says.

"And the time of death?"

He shakes his head. "Too early." He stands and stretches. Then, from a hook near the door, Joe lifts his holstered gun and puts it on. "Now we wait for the forensic reports."

After her father drives off, Kate carries a deck chair out to the shed, sits in the doorway, notebook in hand, and stares at her mother's things, searching for bug colonies — the evidence of movement, of return.

A thick layer of dust covers everything, but as she continues to stare, she sees that the boxes stacked on the two trunks have yellowed to various shades. At first, she assumed that the bottom boxes, being the oldest, would be the deepest yellow. Kate has proof of this in

Rose's basement, where she boxed and stored her own treasures years ago. She has stacked new ones on top, so that the additions complete a chronology, the stages of her life neatly labelled and put to rest. DOLL CLOTHES, YEAR-BOOKS, SENTIMENTAL STUFF, CLASSICAL MUSIC, LETTERS, OLD RECORDS, CHARTS, ENCYCLOPAEDIA BRITANNICA, UNIVERSITY MEMORABILIA. Like digs, the earth strataed with ruins, the oldest often assimilated into the more recent. Like canyon walls, memories.

Focus. The top box has colouring that clearly belongs to the bottom layer. She sees, suddenly, the faint traces of a hand print on its side. She gets up and, without moving the box, opens its lid. Inside are scraps of fabric, jars filled with odd buttons, a chocolate box overflowing with zippers, a large Christmas cookie tin stuffed with slippery silk, a tiny black velvet ring box inside of which is a spool of blue thread.

BLUE THREAD: SEWING BOX 2 [10]

When Iris ran off to Yakima the summer Kate turned one, Joe begged Rose to help him with Kate. Two months later, Iris returned, as abruptly as she'd left, offering no explanation.

By then, Joe and Rose had resigned themselves to Iris' manic days of laughter and Stones music and stilt acrobatics, and to the inevitable depressions that followed — days when Iris would lie in bed or on the couch, comatose, undressed, unwashed, eyes staring at a distant horizon. These "episodes," as Joe called them, occurred every few months.

Rose stayed on for three weeks because although Iris appeared to be perfectly normal, she began to say disturbing things.

"I died as a child."

"My parents were killed and replaced by imposters."

Neither Rose nor Joe could tell whether she was baiting them or truly believed these things.

One morning Iris returned from the market and proudly announced to Rose that she had purchased her first very own spool of thread — the colour of iris, her namesake. She was going to learn how to sew that very afternoon. Almost immediately, she became interested in the orchard, Joe's job, Rose's prospects for a husband, Kate.

While packing to leave, Rose asked Iris if she could borrow the blue thread to sew on a button that had come off her denim shirt.

"ARE YOU CRAZY?" Iris shouted. She clenched her teeth, sprang back, and hopped side to side, like a boxer evading a punch.

"It's all right. It's all right," Rose said softly.

"This spool of thread," Iris whispered, her fist stuffed into the pocket of her jeans, "is *magical*! It gives whoever has it superhuman powers! *I* have to hold it!" She looked around, as if expecting eavesdroppers. Then she patted

Rose's hand. "I'll buy you one of your own, if you like," she said, and smiled.

Joe asked Rose to stay on a few more weeks. It didn't occur to them to find a therapist. Although Iris appeared cheerful, now and then a disturbing anxiety showed through. But there were no more "episodes."

She was, however, increasingly obsessed with the spool of thread. She was terrified to lose it, or even worse, to have someone else use it. She checked it several times a day to make sure the thread was still wound through the slash at the top of the wooden spool.

One evening she found it undone. She rushed downstairs to where Rose was watching TV. "Did you use some of my thread?" she asked, breathless.

"No," Rose said. "What's the matter?"

"You've sewn the button on!" Iris cried, near hysteria.

Rose got up and tried to calm her, but Iris pushed her away. "Iris, I bought some thread of my own. Honest, I didn't take yours."

"I want to see it!" Iris cried. "Show me!"

Rose went to the sewing basket, pulled out a spool of blue thread and held it out. Iris did not touch it. She stood, leaning against the door frame, silent and brooding. Then she went upstairs, after politely bidding Rose good night.

In her room, she sat on the bed, pulled out her own thread and examined it. It was almost full; she might be able to save the magic yet. She decided to eliminate every piece of blue clothing in the house. She began in her own closet and filled a large garbage bag. Then she proceeded to the other rooms, making certain she was quiet, so Rose would not hear her above the trash talk of the TV.

Kate coaxes the blue thread back into its velvet case. She closes the box, slipping each corner under the next, carefully following the old marks. On one side, a neat print: SEWING 2. She searches until she finds two others labelled SEWING 1 and SEWING 3, neither of which has been disturbed. She can assign these boxes a year when they might have been packed: Sept. – Oct. 1966.

Iris did learn how to sew, although by the following August, when Rose returned, Iris had completely forgotten the blue thread and her obsession with it. She had sewn many identical outfits for herself, Kate and her dolls, and for a while, insisted they all dress alike. Kate doesn't recall any of this, so she can only imagine Joe coming home home from work to find them arranged on the couch — Iris, Kate, then a variety of dolls from the largest to the smallest — like the children she'd seen in *The Sound of Music,* only they were all female and dressed in identical clothes. Or Ukrainian dolls fitted one inside the other, Iris' multiple personalities.

In her notebook, Kate writes: SEWING 1, 2 & 3 — 1966+, then she puts the notebook down and carefully inspects the two steamer trunks pushed against the inside wall. She lifts the boxes off them and places them on the floor in the order she found them. She keeps wishing she'd taken photographs before she disturbed anything, though she has her drawing and grid.

She looks again at the trunks now that they're free. Oak and rectangular with rounded edges, one much more worn than the other. Its top is gouged and its brass case corners, hinges, draw catches, loops and pegs are tarnished and scratched, as if the trunk has been dragged across the decks of steamers, stored beneath berths. In the leather handles, she can smell foreign countries. These are the kind of trunks grandmothers keep in the attic, the kind that contain languid dreams of escape. If only Kate could board a slow freighter, wake up near the shore of an exotic island where no one knows her. For a moment it's possible. She could take one of the trunks, dump its contents as she runs, use it as a raft, a magic carpet, something to keep her afloat.

The moment passes.

The boxes and trunks suddenly look mottled with dust, weighed with unbearable grief. Outside, the sun is low in the sky and already, a crispness. She has lost all track of time. Her watch says 6:42. She wonders where Joe and Ray are, whether they're together. She wonders, too, where Angie is, whether she should phone her. Her loyalty branches, its limbs spindly and brittle as dry wood. She lifts out the worn trunk and drags it upstairs to her room. She breaks the lock with a screwdriver, opens the lid. The trunk is lined in cedar, and the inside lid papered in antique flowers.

STEAMER TRUNK I [4]

A smaller box with neatly taped ends fills half the trunk. On its top, in red felt marker, the word IRIS, as if the box might contain her. The other half of the trunk is stacked with loose papers, books, envelopes. Kate opens the box first, lifts out everything and spreads it on the bed. The puzzle pieces of her mother are laid out before her. She has no idea what anything means. She fishes out her notebook and begins to record:

1. GRADE 5 YEARBOOK — autographed by students (1956).
2. ON THE ROAD by Jack Kerouac, first published in 1957, when Iris was eleven.
3. PASSPORT valid until 1970.
4. Happy 14ᵗʰ Birthday! CARD from Oma Hinton.
5. MOTHER–OF–PEARL PIGGY BANK in the shape of a dog.
6. Beat-up SET OF GUITAR STRINGS, in their original paper package.
7. Dark blue PERFUME ATOMIZER: Evening in Paris.
8. SHORTHAND BOOK from senior high.
9. A MORRIS THE CAT CALENDAR with funny pictures and captions, its large squares scrawled with cryptic symbols, hieroglyphics.
10. JOAN BAEZ SONG BOOK.
11. PHOTO OF IRIS as a gawky teenager standing next

to a smiling elderly woman — Iris is grinning
and clutching a guitar in her left hand.
12. DEATH ANNOUNCEMENT: In Loving Memory of
Katerina Hinton, born October 6, 1872. Died
February 10, 1962.
13. NEWSPAPER CLIPPINGS of the Kennedy assassina-
tions and the moon landing.

Kate puts down her pen and rereads what she has
written. It's like hearing a song in a foreign language: you
can intuit the mood, but not the story.

She knows, for example, that Iris idolized her great-
grandmother, Katerina Hinton, who came from Germany
to America as a Hurdy-Gurdy Girl in 1887 — one of
many young women who had been promised employment as a dancer in the gold rush towns of North America.
She was taken to Edmonton, to the Klondike, and there,
she danced in saloons with lonely miners for the price of
a drink, of which she could keep fifty cents. The Hurdy-
Gurdies worked long hours and could not leave their jobs
because their parents had signed contracts that indentured
the girls to their employers until they had repaid their
passage, room and board. Most did as Oma Hinton did —
they married a miner who paid off their debt.

When we were seven or eight, Iris and I would sneak
into the attic and dress up in the costumes Oma had
folded and placed in trunks years before. Iris always

played the Hurdy-Gurdy and me, the miner. We'd play-
act the saloon scenes Oma had described to us, until we
were twirling and jumping, flaying and swaying, giddy
and wild, our faces flushed and moist. Then, our mother
would come up to see what all the noise was about and
order us downstairs to act like ladies.

It was Oma who reassured Iris that bleeding was perfectly
normal, that she'd be doing it once a month and that she
did not have a terrible disease. It was Oma who bought
Iris her first guitar when she was fourteen, who encour-
aged her and paid for guitar lessons. It was Oma who
explained all about sex and french-kissing. And it was
two months after Oma died that Iris left home.

Skeletal remains, Kate thinks, staring at her mother's
amulets. How to identify her? If only each of Elaine's
notes matched a fragment. When she hears the door
open and slam shut downstairs, she quickly puts everything back inside the box, closes the trunk, and throws
a shirt over it.

"Kate?"

"I'm coming," she says and steps out into the hall,
closing the door behind her. She listens for the sound of
other voices.

"There you are," Joe says when she walks into the
kitchen. He has taken a tomato out of the fridge and is
eating it as if it were a ripe juicy fruit, his head bowed
over the sink. Between bites, he salts it.

"I'm worried about Angie," Joe says. "This is really hard on her." He washes his hands in the sink, then runs them, wet, over his face.

"Angie's *alive*," Kate says. "You never worried about Patti. None of us did."

"I was wrong," he says, slowly. "There. Are you satisfied?"

Kate sighs. Her stomach hurts. Every unspoken, unresolved conflict between them is knotted there. She takes another deep breath.

Joe reads her silence as forgiveness. He pats her arm. "Look, could you call Angie?" he says. "She's going to need someone ... Thing is, I may have to pick up Trevor."

"You've got something?"

"Not exactly. But we do have the cause and time of death. A skull fracture, and Trevor was still here."

"When exactly?" she asks.

"The night of the funeral," Joe says. "Sometime between 9:00 p.m. and 1:00 a.m." He pauses. "You didn't see him, did you? On your *drive*, I mean."

Ambush. Subterfuge, subtext. *Did he have someone follow me?*

"I didn't see Trevor," she says, slowly. *Who does he think he is?* "Neither on my drive nor at The Palace, where I stopped for a nightcap." She opens the fridge and takes out the ice-cube tray. Then she slowly mixes herself a drink, her face innocuous.

"With Matt?" His voice is sharp, a scolding-daddy voice.

"What's it to you?" she says. "I'm an adult."

"He has a wife and two small children."

"Who's spying for you? Because if they're any good, you'll know that's all it was — a drink between old friends," she says.

He sighs then, and it makes her think of a live volcano, and how its frequent steams of sighs fool people into thinking it'll never blow.

"I didn't mean to pry, Kate," he says softly.

"Yeah. Maybe you should find Trevor so you can ask *him* where he was."

He opens the door. "No matter what," he says, "Angie had nothing to do with this."

She watches him drive away, a fault line forming in his tracks and she wants to rush out and tell him they are supposed to be on the same side. They are not in one of those fairy tales peopled by motherless girls: Cinderella, Snow White, the Little Match Girl, Gretel, Dorothy, Anne of Green Gables, Beauty, Rupunzel, etc.; they are not in one of those fairy tales in which fathers banish their daughters to save themselves.

"He swears he didn't do it," Angie shouts above the rumble of the grader, "and I believe him." Her arms are crossed, as if she expects Kate will try to stab her.

They're outside, on a makeshift bridge between two trenches next to the trailer. Police cars are parked down by the street, and Kate can see Matt waving on traffic, curiosity-seekers who have come for a better look.

But this is not Graceland or Sharon Tate's house or the Chappaquiddick Island bridge.

"Could we get out of this zoo?" Kate says. "My car's just up the road."

Angie hesitates for a moment, then drops her arms to her sides. "Not for long," she says, and follows Kate out to the car.

Kate heads toward Winthrop, away from the action. Beside them the Methow River drifts through the valley like the trickle of a leaky hose, yielding to trees, rocks, anything in its path. It's hard to imagine the roaring treachery it becomes farther down. *Angie.* She imagines their friendship as a current carving into the course of their lives. It reminds her of a small cove she and Angie went to last year, on the Oregon coast. They were walking on rocky cliffs, along thin cracks, imagining foreign maps, when water spurted out in a sudden burst and drenched them. They laughed, surprised, uneasy that the sea roared beneath their feet.

"Patti told me she wanted to get away from Trevor," Kate says.

Angie keeps her face averted, stares out the window. "Trevor never laid a hand on her," she says, but her voice is not convincing.

Kate clenches the steering wheel. "Like father, like son," she says.

"So he might have lost his temper now and then," Angie says, flippant. "But who doesn't?"

"Angie, please," Kate says, thinking, *The Kaiadilt, the Ik. Violence. Survival.* She wants to shout, *Patti was a teenager in your care.* She wants Angie to admit her son was abusive and she did nothing about it.

Angie turns to her then. "I'm really sorry about Patti," she says. "I had a lot of mixed feelings about her, but I really did care about her. She lived with us for five years, for god's sake. She was like one of mine."

"Then you must want justice," Kate says. She turns left onto a gravel road and stops. "Dad says they're going to pick up Trevor. Why don't you tell them where he is?"

"I *don't know* where he is," Angie says, angry.

Kate stares straight ahead. *Maybe he's in Mexico.* What irony, Patti's father and lover trade places.

"Trevor *didn't do* it," Angie says, stressing the two *d*s, her voice sharp. "That's what he says, and that's good enough for me."

Kate sighs. "You think my father would defend your son even if he's guilty?"

"He's *not* guilty." Angie crosses her arms again. "You don't understand because you don't have any children." She turns her head and stares out the window.

"I don't see what having or not having children has to do with it," Kate says, her voice rising. "Patti was somebody's daughter too."

Angie emits an ugly laugh. "Having second thoughts about that divorce, are you?"

Kate pulls in her breath, as if it's been knocked out of

her. Friendship. *You don't stab in the underbelly.* "We're not talking about my divorce," Kate says. "We're talking about your son killing his girlfriend."

"That's your version."

"Suggest another one. What do you think? Some stranger off the street battled through all that blasted construction, killed Patti for no reason and buried her? Really plausible, Angie."

"Maybe she was involved in something."

"Right," Kate says. "She was involved with your son and she wanted out badly enough to ask for my help. I should have gotten her out of there the first day I saw her."

"I wish you had," Angie says.

They sit for a moment. Kate closes her eyes, tries to visualize something beautiful. *Cool. Snowflakes. Icicles. Blue icebergs brilliant in sun.* Outside, the air is still, not a branch, not a leaf moves. She starts the car, turns it and drives Angie back to the trailer. When she stops, Angie flips the lever, kicks open the door and steps out. "I guess it takes a crisis to see who your friends are," she says and slams the door.

"*You're* no friend!" Kate yells after her, instead of, *Please don't leave.*

~

Twisp, 1966. One night, the winter after Iris came home from Goa, she awakened to a terrible ice storm inside her head. Snowflakes swarmed like flies on tree branches, spiky icicles formed drip by drip — crystal stalactites — in the cave of her brain, lakes froze behind her eyes. When she told Joe about it, he said she'd had a nightmare. But Iris insisted she had not slept at all, that the ice storm was still raging in her head. She felt completely exhausted and couldn't cook dinner.

Joe called the doctor who didn't find anything physically wrong but prescribed tranquilizers. Instead of swallowing them, Iris spat them into a planter, afraid that if sedated, she might freeze in the storm. Ice*wo*man. She languished in the upstairs bedroom, barely able to lift her arm off the bed while Joe phoned a neighbour to come and babysit Kate. Iris lay still, listening to his voice, until she felt weightless, insubstantial.

By the time the neighbour arrived, Iris was no longer inside herself. She observed the objects and the people in the room zoom out, farther and farther, as if she were looking through the wrong end of a telescope.

Her lips swelled and she ran into the bathroom to stare at her face, at her tongue, which felt twisted and paralyzed. But she looked normal. The ice storm swirled in her head, hoarfrost gathered around her thoughts, everything slowly froze until her mind became a silent glacier.

~

Rose arrives, unannounced, on Friday afternoon in the middle of Patti's funeral. She slips into an empty chair in the back row, her silk pink shawl rustling and turning heads. She and Kate greet each other with their eyes. Beside Kate, Ray sits unflinching.

They're gathered at the small chapel. The minister drones on and on about Patti's "contribution to the community and the world at large." *Wasted life.* Kate glances around: most people stare away from the minister, their hands fidgeting. Kate listens to the sound of the minister's voice, a bland, monotonous soulless instrument.

Angie sits across the aisle from them, in the section for Trevor's relatives, her eyes red and watery. Kate feels sorry for her, for the fact that she has to stick up for Trevor, who is still in hiding. Joe sits at the back; Matt stands by the door.

After the service, when they've all filed past the closed coffin, they linger outside like clumps of tumbleweed. Angie speaks to people in low tones, sniffles into a Kleenex. Now and then someone pats her back. Nearby, Trevor's friends, a hive of testosterone — a shuffling, buzzing lot, chained, tattooed and pierced, their breaths blue billows of smoke. To one side, a small police contingent take it all in. Rose chats to someone on the street, next to Joe's car. Kate stands beside Ray, whose silence has settled over them like a pesticide cloud. She makes herself breathe, her lips slightly turned up in what she thinks is an encouraging smile. Ray has insisted that he bury Patti alone and is now impatient for everyone to leave. They are awkward, trying to respect his wishes, but not wanting to abandon him too soon.

Finally, Rose touches the stragglers lightly on the arms and gives a slight nod toward the street, successfully herding them away. Kate follows Ray to the door, but he stops her with a look.

"Will you be all right?" she asks.

"Yes."

"I can wait ... we could —"

"I'm driving out to Pateros," he says. "Joe's got the number."

She hears the dismissal, touches his sleeve. "Take care."

"See you," he says, and goes inside.

When she turns, the street is deserted except for Rose, who sits in her car. It's almost October, Kate thinks, staring at the sun whose brilliance is cool, whose colour is a disguise. She wonders where everyone has gone.

Dear Ms. Mason,

I knew an Iris Mason in Yakima back in 1965. I was waitressing with her at the Blue Note Café, I believe, though she wasn't there very long. We spent a bit of time together, so if you think this is the person you're looking for, please call me at 952-2621. Thank you.

Sophia Skofinski

When she wakes up Saturday morning it's still dark. She knows it's too early to wake Rose, but she's anxious to speak to her, to show her the treasures in the trunk.

She turns on the bedside lamp, gets up and carefully clears the table of the quilt, making sure all the parts stay together. She has finished stitching together the blocks. Of the nine squares that make up each block, only three are whole. The rest are sectioned into triangles within triangles so that she has had to sew together forty-two pieces to make each block. She loves the symmetry of it, the ease with which the design emerges.

At the Twisp library the other day, she looked up the pattern in a quilt book. Cat's Cradle: "The six diagonal designs are meant to cause movement across the quilt's surface." She looked up "cat's cradle" in the dictionary, to see if it had another meaning.

CAT'S CRADLE (1768)
1 : a game in which a string looped in a pattern like a

178

*cradle on the fingers of one person's hands is transferred
to the hands of another so as to form a different figure
2 : something that is intricate, complicated, or elaborate.*

She opens the trunk and spreads the contents of the box
on the table, in approximate chronological order, beginning with the yearbook: 1956, the year Elvis Presley
seduced a continent of teenagers with his "Heartbreak
Hotel," "Blue Suede Shoes" and gyrating hips; the year
Queen Elizabeth II opened Calder Hall, Britain's first
atomic power station; the year of "happiness pills" —
tranquilizers whose prescriptions could be continually
refilled. *Mostly by women.* She wonders if Iris went to
school sock-hops and kissed boys in the back seats of
powder-blue Chevys. When Kate was fourteen, she and
Matt made out on the L.A. Freeway, a dirt road at the
end of a straight stretch on Highway 48. Once, when
Matt's car wouldn't start, they had to walk the three miles
back to town, back to an angry, anxious Joe.

When she has strategically arranged all the objects
on the table, like toy soldiers, it's still only 5:40 a.m. She
clasps on Iris' rhinestone bracelet, lies back on the bed,
and raises her arm to the light. The bracelet's metal is
tarnished, but the stones glitter in prisms on the walls —
fireflies flitting from place to place. She wonders if
fireflies' lights go out in the day like dusk-to-dawn porch
lights, and how it would feel to never have night.

By the time she finally gets Rose to herself, it's past

noon. Joe hung around all morning, hoping they'd ask him to join them in the exploration of the trunk. But today Kate wants Rose to herself, wants her to know that Iris could never replace her.

Rose picks up the birthday card, the photo and Oma's death announcement, and looks at each for a moment before handing them to Kate.

"All I know is somebody was messing with Iris, and Oma Hinton put a stop to it," Rose says. "Iris wouldn't say who it was."

Were there uncles? Cousins? Once Iris left home, she no longer had a family. It's impossible to shut out the past, move to a new city, clean slate, start over. *Herstory.* Kate is missing all the motherline stories — those maps other women use to track their own journeys, maps that offer guidance, caution, reassurance. She rubs the front of the birthday card, voicing her thoughts.

"If Iris had been there when you were growing up," Rose says, eyebrows raised, "you probably wouldn't have listened, anyway." She smiles. "When we're young, we think we know better. Besides, what would be the point? We need to discover things for ourselves." She lies back on the bed and stares up at the ceiling. "If I'd done everything my mother did, I'd be her, not me." She rolls onto her side, takes Kate's hand. "You've done all right, Kate. Don't make your mother into something she isn't, and don't regret anything."

Kate puts the items back in the box along with the

guitar strings, the newspaper clippings, the perfume bottle and the Joan Baez songbook. She wonders if Iris still plays guitar. She wonders who Iris is now. *Until I know where Iris is, I won't get ....* The word *"closure"* springs out of a New Age doublespeak. *Closure*, Kate thinks, imagining doors slamming, coffins nailed down, nuns cloaked and habited, Alzheimer's patients whose memories are a series of shutters closing, closing. No, closure is not what she wants. She wants aperture — a window, a door, her eyes, mind, opening until she can see Iris, mother, self.

All afternoon, Kate and Rose sift through the rest of the items, but find Elaine has written little or nothing about them. No mention of the perfume bottle, the passport. The mother-of-pearl piggy bank sat on Iris' dresser and was bought at a seaside town one holiday. Iris saved the cat-food labels, then sent away for Morris the Cat calendars, which she tacked to the wall and scribbled in daily, in an invented language. Kate repacks all these in the box, thinking it's what's *not* said she yearns for.

She recalls what she has squirreled away over the years: a small notebook with a silk Chinese cover of dragons in green and gold. Someone finding it would see an exquisite hand-sewn book, pages pristine; might not notice twelve of them are missing. The book was a gift from Stephen. On those pages, she'd composed sentimental overwrought poems about their love affair. When they broke up, she carefully ripped out the pages, pulled out the corresponding ones at the back, and burned them ceremoniously in the bathroom sink. She flushed the ashes down the toilet.

Now she hands Rose the last thing on the bed, a red steno pad whose right-hand corner curls up like a sneer. The brittle, yellowy pages are wide ruled and have no margins except for a thin green line down the middle. Rose flips it open and reads some of the shorthand for a moment, then laughs.

"What does it say?" Kate asks.

"Gobbledygook. This isn't shorthand." Rose slams the page shut.

Kate opens the book at random and points to the curlicues. "What are those, then?"

Rose shakes her head. "Some game, maybe? Who knows?"

Kate thinks about all that's lost in childhood — toys, drawings, poems, paper hearts and Mother's Day cards, diaries, letters — all that evidence of intense emotions precisely articulated, and how jumbled it becomes through the years, and easily abandoned, like faulty appliances on Sally Ann shelves. This loss, however, translates into the freedom to reinvent one's childhood and those of one's children. Her friends back in the city own videocams and have scrupulously used them since their babies were born. Imagine those children as adults, able to view their carefully documented lives on video clips. There'll be no revisionist memories, no claims of happiness or sorrow that the lens has not captured. They will know exactly how clever or how stupid they were as children, how apt to do this or that. There will be no imagining possible, no myth-making, no sentimental journey.

Early Sunday morning, Kate helps Rose pack for her trip home.

"I'd like to stay," she says. "But work calls ...." She hugs Kate, then climbs into the car and cinches her seat belt.

Kate closes the door and leans on the open window, holding out the photograph she found in Iris' skirt pocket. "Do you know who this is?" she asks, handing Rose the photo. "Is he the man she ran off with?"

Rose studies the face for a moment, then shakes her head. "The last time I saw Iris was the fall of 1966, a good year before she left for good." She shrugs and hands back the photo.

"I'll see you soon," Kate says.

"If you really want to know, ask your dad."

Kate stiffens. "He's hardly ever told me anything about her. And what he has, turns out to be lies."

"Maybe you should try again." Rose shifts into gear and elbows Kate's arms off the window. Kate watches her car until it blends into the foliage of the orchard.

The rest of the morning Kate sews Elaine's quilt. She has begun to join the finished patchwork to the solid black background, working slowly to keep the two fabrics smooth. At night, she lays it over her on the bed, unfinished.

A little past noon, she quits sewing and goes out to the shed. Inside the baby carriage, she finds her doll.

DOLL WITH CRACKED HEAD: BABY CARRIAGE [11]

The year Iris returned from Goa, when she made Kate and her dolls wear dresses identical to hers, Rose came to visit and brought Kate a doll with a hard straw body, soft plastic limbs and a porcelain head. Kate adored the doll, particularly because her eyes closed when she laid her down. A mystery — how the smallest tilt of the head made her succumb to sleep, while her mother lay for hours stretched on the couch, eyes staring through the wall of their house. Sometimes, Kate would run her hand over her mother's forehead, over her eyes, like Joe sometimes did at night. Like they do for the dead. But her mother's eyes remained open, unblinking.

One day, to discover how her doll's eyes worked, Kate took her outside, laid her on a stump, picked up a stone and smashed in her skull. A chunk fell out, intact, jagged, like the top of an eggshell. She picked up the doll and looked inside at the heavy metal arm that weighed the eyes shut. She held the end of it and moved the doll so that the eyes remained open. It didn't seem so mysterious and magical any more. If only she could lower her mother's lids, hide the terrible absence in her eyes.

When she looked up, her mother's ghost face pressed against the window. Kate turned her back to hide the doll, which now looked grotesque, her forehead ragged as if her skull had been devoured by some wild creature. Kate quickly set her down, found a piece of bark and wedged it under the metal arm. She abandoned the doll on the stump, eyes staring up.

Late that night, she was awakened by her mother, who gathered her up out of bed and put her in the car. "It's all right, Darling," Iris said. "Everything's fine." She backed the car out all the way to the highway without turning on the lights. Kate fell asleep against her arm.

She awakened when the car door opened, and light shone on her mother's nightgown, her bare feet, her wide gaping eyes. It was dark, still.

Kate started to cry.

Her mother was stroking a bundle wrapped in a silk shawl. "Hush, now," she said. "We're here." From the trunk, she took a spade. Then she pulled Kate by the hand along a path flanked by tall menacing figures and shadows.

Presently, she turned. "Look," she said. "This is where dead people live." She bent down and rubbed one of the headstones. "We'll all be here one day. The Lost and Found." She laughed and held out her hand.

Kate shrank from her. The Everlasting Kingdom was supposed to be a happy, busy place up in the sky, not here in the dark and cold.

"Come along," her mother said, her voice brusque, practical. "There's nothing to be afraid of."

Kate stumbled behind her.

Soon Iris stopped, put down the bundle and began to dig. Kate watched, shivering. Then, the flicker of light toward them. Her mother looked up, stricken. She threw the spade aside, lifted the bundle and gently placed it in the hole.

Kate heard her father call, "Iris!" and "Kate!" and she cried out his name, even though her mother was whispering, "*Shhhhh. Shhhhhhh.*"

Then Joe was beside them and she was in his arms and he was pulling her mother by the hand, saying, "For god's sake, Iris. For god's sake," in a voice both shocked and frightened.

On Monday morning, Kate awakens to the doll on her bedside table, split skull facing her. She turns off the alarm, hugs the doll, then sniffs the stuffing. Mildew, nothing else. *How did this end up with Iris' things?* And why did Iris leave behind all the signposts of her youth? ... *I'm going to cut ties ....* Start over. What would happen if Kate were to suddenly disappear? Would anyone search for her?

Last night, she phoned Ray and asked if she could stop by today, on her way home from Yakima. She didn't explain about Sophia Skofinski, the ads in the papers, the inheritance, Iris. Instead, she said she had an appointment.

"I'll be apple-picking till dark," he said.

She understood his return to work; better than sitting in the house alone, surrounded by absence. "I probably wouldn't get there till dark myself," she told him.

"I'll see you then," he said.

Now as she turns onto the highway, she imagines Ray doing the same, the two of them driving toward each other as if this were the ending of a sentimental movie. *Dream on, dreamscape, dreamland, dream time, dreamboat, dream world, dreamer.* Ray has a Mexican girlfriend — she will not get caught in the webbed hoop of any dreamcatcher and dissipate at dawn.

In Yakima, after lunch, Kate parks in front of the three-storey building where Sophia Skofinski lives in a two-bedroom condo with her daughter and grandson.

She's a small, plump woman with ruddy skin, streaked blonde hair, and large blue, tired eyes. "Come in. Come in." She clears toys off the couch and waves Kate onto it. "My daughter was called in to work, so I've got Joey." The toddler looks at her unsteadily, then begins to howl. "*Shhh. Shhhh,*" Sophia says. She picks him up and bounces him in her arms. "See the doggie out there? Look. Look at the doggie."

Kate stares at the chaos children create, thinking how difficult it must be to care for a child at Sophia's age. Shouldn't Sophia be on adventure treks and Caribbean cruises? Studying for university degrees and gardening exams? She wonders if there is a husband somewhere.

"Do you drink coffee? Or tea, maybe? There must be some tea around here. Me, I hardly ever drink it."

"Coffee's fine," Kate says. On the table in front of her are several photo albums.

"Good. I just made some before you came." She marches to the island between the kitchen and the living room, takes out mugs, fills them, puts them on a tray and carries it in with one hand, while the other supports the child straddling her hip.

"You said you knew my mother," Kate says, anxious. "Are you in touch with her?"

Sophia shakes her head. "Like I said, I *think* I knew your mother ... at least, I worked with somebody called Iris Mason, years ago. I've been going through the albums, because I know we took a picture of the whole gang. Somebody's birthday party after-hours. Once the till was done, we'd sit around until three, four in the morning."

She puts the baby on the floor amid the toys and flips through a few pages of one album, moves to the middle, then the back. "It's before this. It must have been back in ... oh I'd have been twenty-one or twenty-two ... no, wait, I didn't come to Yakima till September ... more like twenty-four, yeah. That makes it '64. Jesus, that sounds like a long time ago." She flips through another album.

Kate sips coffee and waits for Sophia to find the photo. When she does, she slides it across to Kate. "Look at us! We thought we were really something." She laughs. The toddler looks up and hurls a plastic ball across the room.

Kate stares at the photo. All the women are in black mini-dresses with frilly white aprons tied at the waist; all the men wear black pants and white shirts. They don't look as stiff as their clothing, though. Some sit, some stand, some squat in front, arms around each other.

"There." Sophia points at the laughing young woman, unmistakably Iris.

"That's her," Kate says.

"That's what I thought." She settles back in the couch, coffee cup in hand.

Kate leans forward, her lungs expanding into the beginning of hysteria. Why didn't she prepare a list of questions? It reminds her of the summer she and Stephen were together, when they were making plans for the future, the way lovers do, without dates, times or commitments — raven-haired twins who would be brilliant surgeons, or a family of ten, perhaps, all of them living in Zanzibar and swimming in moonlight.

She began to type out a list of questions for her mother and/or anyone who knew her, pent-up questions like: "What did Iris *do* when she saw me after an absence?" Or "How did Iris feel about herself?" Or "How was her pregnancy and labour with me?" Or "Did she ever say she loved me?" It seemed extremely important that she know these things before she married Stephen.

Of course, she never married Stephen.

She wonders now if it was she who orchestrated those fantasies, and whether Stephen had simply played along, like an actor under her direction. "What do you remember about her?" she says, now. "Anything. I was too small when she left."

Sophia frowns. "Yeah, I knew she had a baby back home. She'd run away or something."

Kate tenses. "She left me with my dad."

"Oh, I'm sorry ...." Sophia looks at her, uncomfortable.

"It's all right," Kate says. "It was a long time ago."

"Well, I don't know if I should tell you this ... like you say, it was a long time ago ...." She sips her coffee, hesitant.

Kate leans forward. "Please."

"Well, like I said, Iris had run away and if you think about it, women didn't do that sort of thing back then." She pauses. "Iris fell madly in love with my ex-husband, Paul, who also worked at the restaurant." She points to a young man in the photo. "That's Paul there, see? I think Iris was married to someone much older."

"Eight years," she says. "My dad's eight years older than she is. That's not a lot."

"It is when you're young."

Kate looks at the photo again and now she senses an intimacy between her mother and the young man — something in the way their shoulders touch, their mouths laugh near each other. "Did they have an affair?" she asks.

"Mind if I smoke?" Sophia gets up.

Kate does, but it's not her house. She shakes her head.

Sophia takes a pack of Camels off the TV set. She shakes the pack against her hand until a cigarette falls out. Unfiltered. She lights it slowly and drags on it before coming back to the couch. "Paul and me, we'd gotten married right out of high school and by the time Iris came along, we were experimenting ... with sex ... open marriage, you know." She looks at Kate, somewhat embarrassed. "We were so young and it was an exciting time ... I suppose that seems strange now." Sophia smiles.

"Not so strange," Kate says. "Some battles are still raging." Rose's yearly list surfaces: 1964, the year the Civil Rights Act extended equal opportunities for women in employment and education; the year three men working for the Congress of Racial Equality were murdered in Mississippi, and Dr. Martin Luther King, Jr. was awarded the Nobel Peace Prize; the year of the Mustang, Teflon, *Mary Poppins*; the year the word "endangered" came into use.

"Every few months," Sophia tells her, "Paul would bring someone home, and she'd stay a while. When I thought about it later, I realized I'd never brought a man home. So our 'open marriage' really was about Paul having new women to sleep with."

"And my mother ... was part of this?" Kate asks. It seems impossible that she is sitting in this conservative living room, discussing Iris' sex life with a complete stranger.

"Well," Sophia says, "I don't exactly know how he convinced her, but one night, there she was." She bends down and pushes a yellow plastic car toward the toddler.

"How long did it last?'

Sophia sighs. She butts out her cigarette. "Three, four weeks, max. Iris wasn't the type, you know?" She sits on the floor with the toddler.

"What happened to your husband?" Kate asks. "Is he still around?"

"No. Not for years," she says, and laughs. "I got smart eventually, dumped him. But I've been married twice since." She stands again. "You want more coffee?"

She nods. "You didn't keep in touch with Iris?"

Sophia pours the coffee and comes back into the living room. "Iris went back to her husband in Twisp. We wrote to each other for a while, but we lost touch ... I don't know what happened, really ... but Iris ended up going abroad. One of the waitresses had relatives abroad. I think they went together."

The trunks. Goan adventure. "Can you point her out?" Kate picks up the photo album and offers it to Sophia.

Sophia looks at the photo for a moment, then shakes her head. "I didn't know her very well," she says. "And to tell you the truth, I can't even picture her right now. As you can see, there were a lot of us. Some were better friends than others. She might have quit by the time this picture was taken." She pushes the album aside. "Me, I stayed on at the restaurant till last year. Took early retirement."

"Iris came back after she'd been abroad. Goa," Kate says, hoping this will help Sophia remember the woman's name.

The best Sophia can do is to call the restaurant to see if they still have employee records from 1964. They don't. She promises to call if she has any leads.

By the time Kate leaves it's after four. It'll take her three, three-and-a-half hours to get to Pateros. She drives slowly, to give Ray time to wash and eat before she gets there.

When she drives up to the cabin, it's dark, but the

porch light is on and he's crouched on the top step, a plate balanced on his knees. He looks up when he sees her and sets the plate down, but doesn't stand. He looks drawn, the overhead light accentuates his cheekbones, the depth of his eye sockets. He's thinner than she remembers; the black T-shirt outlines his ribs, blends him into the night.

"Hey," she says at the bottom of the steps. She hands him the bag of doughnuts she bought on the way. His favourites: banana cream, jelly, plain.

He takes the bag but doesn't look inside. "How you doing?"

She sits on the steps. "Fine. You?" Words stick in her throat. She swallows.

He stands and picks up his plate. "You want a beer?" he asks.

"Sure." It seems absurd that they can't talk. She thinks about last summer, the night they dragged the mattress out and lay on it, naked, in moonlight. Ray said that without the moon, the Earth would flop around, pulled this way and that by the capricious magnetic fields of the other planets. They imagined what it would be like to have darkness for a year — all vegetation dead — or scorching summer — the valley a yellow desert, the river dry. They imagined polar bears or tigers rooting in their back yards. They imagined the population of the world huddling together on any continent that could support life. They imagined technophiles trying to create a new moon. They made love, thankful to be right where they were, grateful for the fragile balance that kept them upright.

Ray comes back with two cans of beer, opens both, and sets them on the porch between them. He sits beside her, elbows on his knees, hands dangling in front. There's paint in the cuticles around his nails, as well as splotches on his jeans and T-shirt.

"Painting again?" she asks.

"I never stopped."

She never went to see his place in Mexico. *I didn't pay enough attention.* Does he draw first, then paint? Does he work from a small sketch? She lets a couple of minutes pass, listens to the rushing Methow nearby before she says, "Any news?"

"Haven't found Trevor yet. Bastard." He swigs his beer, wipes his mouth on his arm. "Did you know he was roughing her up?"

Kate bites her lip. "Not really," she says, hesitant. "I wasn't there two days before she ... disappeared ...." She turns and stares at the horizon.

Beside her, Ray bristles, quill by quill, as if he were readying for combat. She stares straight ahead, swallows; the air tastes murky with anger.

"You waited a week to tell me she was missing?" Ray's voice is tight, raging.

"I didn't know," Kate says, her own voice rising in tandem. "I was out of town and when I got back, I phoned you immediately. Not that you got on a plane right away." She takes a deep breath.

They sit in silence. Finally, Ray says, "I'm sorry. I didn't mean to —"

"No, *I'm* sorry," Kate says, quickly. "It's not your fault. There's nothing you could have done."

Ray sucks in his breath, and Kate thinks she'll burst into tears if he says anything at all. She picks up the bag of doughnuts and stands. "I'll get a plate," she says, and pushes against the door.

Ray turns quickly. She can tell by his face that he wants to prevent her from going inside. He opens his mouth, then shuts it.

Ray has altered the largest mural, *The Day of the Dead — City Fiesta.* Gone are the drinks and food, the raucous faces. All the people in the foreground now face the figures of death on stage, their backs curved and introspective. Only one woman, in the bottom right-hand corner, stares out of the mural, careless and detached. She is wearing Kate's face. Kate is stunned. Is this how he sees her? She hurries past the mural, into the kitchen, tears welling. She takes a plate out of the cupboard, and it's too familiar. She sits down, head on the table, and cries.

Ray does not come in after her.

When she's back in control, she goes to the bathroom, washes her face, then takes the doughnuts outside. Ray has finished his beer. He looks up at her, but in the shadows, he can't possibly see the red circling her eyes. Neither mentions the mural.

As soon as she sits down, he gets up. "Want another one?" he asks, holding up the can.

"Hardly had a sip of this one," she says. While he's inside, she goes to the car and gets her sweater. Each night, a little cooler.

Ray flicks off the porch light before he comes back out. For a moment, she's blinded by the intense black. Then her eyes slowly adjust. Ray sits beside her. He opens the can with the whoosh of a spirit escaping. She read once that Frederick II used to lock up convicts in an airtight room until they suffocated, in order to watch their souls escape when he opened the door.

She tells him about Elaine, Iris, Rose. He listens without interrupting, murmuring to encourage her. She can't see his face in the darkness.

"I hope you find your mother," he says when she has finished. "It'll be the end of something."

The end of something.

"What'll happen to Patti's baby?" she asks Ray.

He shrugs. "We haven't talked about it yet. Angie and me. I could take her, I suppose." He drops his head in his hands. "Déjà vu. I've already done this." He turns to her, concealed, intense. "I just don't know if I'm up to it."

She touches his hand.

"I don't know what's worse," he says. "Your life stretched out in front of you, or a big gate slammed shut."

They look out across the valley and, in the dark, it sprawls boundless, borders undefined by ownership or fences. In the distance, a stream of headlights — cars on the highway — a boundary forcing the eye to stop.

She tells Ray about the Tasaday tribe in the Philippines who, until the 1970s, were isolated in the mountains of Mindanao. They called the edge of the forest "the place where the eye sees too far." They were frightened by it. She tells him that when John Nance, a reporter and photographer, first saw them in 1971, they came out of the forest and one of them said, "I think we're going to die."

"And did they?" he asks.

"Not physically, but some of their culture did. In order to survive, they had to change, to assimilate."

"The place where the eye sees too far," Ray says. "Maybe we're better off not looking. Isolated."

"Is that why you go to Mexico?" she asks.

He doesn't reply for a moment. She listens to the river nearby. "It's a *kind* of isolation," he says, cautious.

Last summer in Pateros, after the nasty quarrel between Ray and Patti, Kate sat on this porch, struggling to forgive Ray for being selfish, for choosing her over Patti, for being exactly like Joe. Yet he had picked *her*.

When he returned, he was fierce and silent. He walked past her into the house and slammed the door. She sensed the ambiguity of his feelings toward both her and Patti. She wondered how Joe must have felt after she and Matt eloped. Her father's rejection had always seemed final. She had never imagined him in turmoil after he left her at Rose's and returned home to Elaine.

When Kate left Ray and returned to Vancouver, she felt as if she had been hurled into a black-and-white moral lesson. How could she love Ray and despise her own father? The more she thought about it, the more grey everything became. Child Kate wanted to hate Ray; adult Kate wanted to curl herself into the hollow of his chest. She paced around the airport, in a state of panic, phoned her father from a pay phone, but his voice pitched her back to the present and she hung up, unnerved. She couldn't love Ray, she decided, any more than she could reinvent her past. She'd have to reassess every choice she ever made, and blame herself for so many failures of the heart. So she did the cowardly thing, phoned Stephen and arranged to see him. "For old times' sake," she said. She went to his office, locked the door and fucked him with few preliminaries. A desperate way to save herself, to detach herself from Ray.

~

In the Amazon jungle, in the inaccessible rainforest near the border with Peru, in unexplored pockets of the Amazon basin, live Brazil's last remote indigenous peoples — as many as twenty-one tribes — people who have had no interaction with the modern world. They are monitored and protected by Brazil's Department of Isolated Indians. When a new tribe is found, government agents mark off its territorial boundaries, then erect guard posts to keep out intruders. They believe this is the only way to save them from extinction. To save them through isolation.

ISOLATION: I. Solo. Quarantine for your own protection.

LOVESICK: a terminal longing, an infestation of memories.

LOVESTRUCK: lips, hands, eyes, words.

LOVELORN: a desolate winter, a singularity — that point in space-time when matter is infinitely dense.

~

Rain drizzles grey and steady on the windshield. Kate is in Seattle, butterflies in her stomach, to see Miranda Magos, who went with Iris to Goa.

Kate did not tell her father where she was going, only that she'd be back in a few days.

She has arranged to meet Miranda Magos at 7:30 for supper at The Green Gourmet. She checks into a hotel around the corner, showers and walks over a little early. She orders a scotch, thinking she'll drink it before Miranda gets there, but Miranda arrives early. She's stunning — tall, slender, elegant — in a navy silk pantsuit and white scooped-neck T-shirt. She walks like a model, shoulders squared, back straight. Her hair is streaked blond and cut very short. She wears sapphire studs in her ears and red lipstick on a generous mouth. She must be fifty or so but looks younger than a lot of forty-somethings. She looks as Kate imagines Iris must.

Her hand is firm in Kate's, and her smile genuine. The waiter sets Kate's scotch in front of her and, before she can begin to make excuses, Miranda says, "I'll have one too," and sits down. She sets a briefcase on the floor beside her.

They chat, order dinner, eat slowly, drink easily. Miranda tells Kate she's a dentist, but when she met Iris in Yakima, she was a waitress saving money to go to Goa, to board with her aunt in Panaji and attend university. On hearing "Goa," Iris became fascinated. She gathered travel brochures, searched in the library encyclopaedias for photos. Miranda told her about Anjuna, the beach town at the edge of the Arabian Sea where scores of hippies had converged to live in "peace, love and a vast selection of hallucinogenics," Miranda says, and laughs. "A global commune."

"Chemical paradise," Kate says.

"It was what she'd always wanted to do," Miranda says. "Try on a different life." She sips her scotch. "But Iris was destined to be unhappy; she was too idealistic, too romantic and impractical."

"That's what everybody says about her."

"Well, you can imagine her in 1964 in small-town America."

Twisp, 1964. Within two weeks of her return from Yakima, ice crystals began to cluster in the creases of Iris' brain. She exploded into tantrums and imploded into frigid storms. On good days, she begged Joe to take her on small trips — anywhere. She yearned for action, change. People her age tramped around North America, hitchhiked across Europe, yogaed through India, barefoot, wooden beads clanking around their necks, idealism scorched into their placid eyes. Iris sat in the house by the river, wishing she could raft the whitewater right out to the Pacific.

In spring, when she heard Joe mention Grand Coulee Dam, she begged him to take her to see it. It sounded immense — 550 feet high and 4173 feet long, important — *power* production flood *control*, river *regulation*. It sounded magnificent, exotic — *Grand* Canyon, *Grand* Canal, *Grand* Prix, *Grand* Coulee Dam. She was intrigued; someone had altered the flow of nature.

Iris looked up the word "coulee" in the dictionary:

COULEE \'kü-lē\ *n* [CanF *coulée*, fr. F, flowing, flow of lava, fr. *couler* to flow, fr. OF, fr. L *colare* to strain, fr. *colum* sieve] (1807)
1   a : a small stream
    b : a dry streambed
    c : a usu. small or shallow ravine: gully
2 : a thick sheet or stream of lava

How could a small stream be like a dry streambed? How could a shallow ravine be like a thick sheet of lava?

"She met Danny at the dam," Miranda says and peers at Kate. "You *do* know about Danny?"

Kate starts to nod, but Miranda sees the lie in her eyes. "I don't really know if I should be telling you this," she says, slicing into an avocado on her vegetarian plate.

"If I could find her, I suppose she'd tell me herself." Kate spears a tomato, then signals the waiter for another round.

Iris met Danny at the dam. She paid fifty cents for the tour while Joe stayed in the car with Kate. At the end of the hour and a half, Iris emerged, stunned. "The minute I saw him," she wrote Miranda in a letter, "I knew I'd married the wrong man."

"Danny was not like your father," Miranda says. "That's probably what attracted her to him." She pauses, daintily dabs her mouth. "There she is, stifled housewife meets bad-boy, you know, an *enfant terrible*." She laughs. "These types were a lot more popular back then, or at least there were more of them —"

"They're still pretty popular," Kate says.

"... and, just like that," Miranda snaps her fingers, "Iris leaves her husband and child to go off with him."

"I thought she went to Goa with you, because you had relatives there," Kate says, startled.

Miranda waves her arm. "Yes, sure, that's true. But Danny came with us."

At the end of summer in 1965, Iris packed one suitcase, scribbled Joe a note, "Don't try to find me," and, with

Miranda, hitchhiked to Seattle, where Danny waited. She had her savings — four hundred and twenty dollars — and the three hundred dollars she took out of their joint account before leaving. The three of them boarded a passenger liner bound for India.

From Bombay, Miranda, Iris and Danny wandered two hundred miles south to Goa, their savings dispersed along dusty roads and yellow beaches. Danny let his hair grow, bought thongs and caftans and gave away his Western clothing. Iris burned her bras on a beach, submerged herself in the lukewarm waters of the Arabian Sea and re-christened herself Liberty. They joined clumps of hippies for yoga and meditation sessions. They bought beads at markets and strung them into necklaces and bracelets. They smoked marijuana and hashish, dropped acid, ate psilocybin mushrooms. They drank unpasteurised milk, ate at roadside stands and, by the time they reached Panaji where Miranda's aunt lived, Iris was vomiting and dehydrated. Miranda's aunt called in a doctor who prescribed antibiotics.

Two weeks later, Miranda pressed her aunt's phone number into Iris' hand and made her promise to return to visit. Iris and Danny continued south another twelve miles to Anjuna, where they finally settled, caught in the midst of an everlasting psychedelic party. When they ran out of money, they bartered their possessions, one at a time. They were joyous, carefree, permanent tourists.

Miranda unzips her briefcase and retrieves a packet of

photos. "Still in the original packaging," she says. "Shows how often I look at them." She puts the orange packet down. "I brought these to show you," she says. "There aren't many ... but it'll give you an idea." She slides the photos out and comments on each. "There. That's my aunt's house. Taken the day we arrived. That's Iris. And that's Danny."

Kate stares at the young man, recognizes Danny from the photo she found in the pocket of Iris' taffeta skirt. "Do you know his last name? Where he's from?"

"Gomez. Danny Gomez. Iris thought it was a movie-star name." She smiles. "As to where he was from — I think someplace near the dam. Can't recall exactly. Moses Lake, maybe?"

Kate thumbs through all the photos, stares at the radiant couple as if they were actors set against the blue walls of the Sahyadris mountains, teetering at the rim of the Aguada headland, seated beside the Talpona River, in the dense mixed jungles of Ravona Dongor. *The Goan Queen.*

"Could I make copies of these?" she asks Miranda. There are negatives in the packet.

"Sure." Miranda pushes her plate aside. "I could use a smoke," she says. "Actually, I quit last year."

Kate smiles. "There's a lounge at my hotel," she says. "Let's go there."

They pay the bill and walk around the corner.

"You know about the baby, of course," Miranda says in the darkness.

The evening air is cool, sudden in Kate's throat. "They had a baby?"

Miranda breathes in, then slowly exhales through tightened lips. "I can't believe nobody told you this."

Iris conceived almost immediately and, for a few months, she and Danny were ecstatic. When she started to show, however, Danny grew moody and irritable. He was too young to be a father, he told her, to be tied to one woman. Free love, he said, was without boundaries, without jealousies. He took off his clothes and stayed stoned for days on end, sampling women in the spirit of freedom and self-expression. Iris sobbed, pleaded, threatened and, ultimately, languished in a hammock until he returned, reeking of incense and musty sex.

"When she was eight months gone, Danny left her in Goa," Miranda says, "and came back to the U.S. Iris came to stay with me and my aunt until she had the baby." She pauses. "A boy."

They've arrived at the lounge. Kate holds the door open for Miranda, then follows her to a booth against the window. Miranda buys a pack of cigarettes, taps out a couple and offers Kate one. She accepts, already dizzy with information.

"So. What happened to the baby?" Kate asks after they've ordered two Spanish coffees. She knows her mother returned to live with them the summer of 1966. She has seen the steamer trunks, the passenger lists.

Miranda draws delicately on the cigarette, inhaling the

smoke so her chest rises, before she slowly exhales a thin trickle of bluish air. "Iris wrote me all about it. Horrible," she says.

Seattle, 1966. The first thing Iris did when she landed in Seattle, the newborn baby in her arms, was to phone Joe. She was wearing a mint seersucker halter dress, as if she'd forgotten that in this hemisphere it's still cool in April.

"Iris?" Joe said. "Iris, where are you?"

The baby began to fret. Iris balanced the receiver between her head and shoulder, and loosened the shawl. His pink, chubby arms beat the air. She smiled, astonished by his miniature hands, his tiny perfect nails. "I want to come home," she said to Joe. "I'll explain everything." She told him about Danny and the baby.

There were lines in the sand, Joe told her, and she had crossed them all. He was right, of course. She listened to him chant her litany of sins: her escape to Goa, her abandonment of Kate, of him, her sordid encounters, her married men, her one-night stands at cheap motels, her drunkenness, her affairs with his friends, his acquaintances, his enemies. But not this. "I won't raise your bastard child," he said. "You come back if you like. Alone."

She phoned her parents next. Her father yanked the phone out of her mother's hands and said, "I have no daughter."

She sat on a chair and breast-fed the baby. She took stock: she had abandoned her parents, her husband, her daughter, as well as various jobs and friends. Survival tactics. Adaptation. For a moment, she wondered what would happen if she simply put down the baby and walked away. Someone would care for him. She got up, laid the sleeping infant in her warm seat and walked to the public phones. She called Joe again, and when he would not relent, slammed the receiver on the hook as hard as she could.

She had no one else to call.

"So she put the baby up for adoption?" Kate says. "Do you know where?"

Miranda shakes her head. "I stayed on in Goa for five years after Iris left. She sent me one letter and that was it. I wrote several times, but she never replied. When I got back, I tried to find her, but her husband — your dad — told me she'd left again." She shrugs and stubs out her cigarette.

"Maybe she went back to Goa," Kate says.

"I don't think so." Miranda signals for a refill. "Like I said, I stayed on, and I've been back several times since. Iris never contacted me or my aunt. She would have at least done that."

After Kate has walked Miranda to her car, she climbs the stairs to her room and paces. Her first impulse is to phone Joe — no matter that it's almost 2:00 a.m. — and yell at him. How could he force Iris to abandon a newborn? Where is the child now? *That night, the bundle in the shawl. Her doll, of course. Yes, of course.* She opens the mini-bar and takes out a scotch. Pours it neat into a glass and downs it.

She lies on the bed and stares at a fixed point, trying to still the swirling in her brain like a ballerina avoiding dizziness when she pirouettes. Balance, balance. Her father will never volunteer information about her mother, she realizes. He is ashamed of Iris, or perhaps he's ashamed that he continued to love her no matter what she did. If only he could tell Kate the truth, rather than protect her from the past, those prisms of events and locations linked by her mother's presence.

She is reminded of a project she worked on in Maryland, to unearth Providence, a town believed to be the first European settlement in the U.S. In just six house sites, they found ceramics from Portugal, Italy and Spain, bricks and tiles from Holland, tobacco pipes and leaded windows from England, wine glasses from Venice. This does not imply wild spending throughout Europe, but rather that a series of travellers had stopped there and traded their goods. Their presence, the link.

I'm following Iris' tracks, she thinks. Like absence, presence, too, can be solidified.

In the morning, she drives home to Vancouver, to her new apartment. She has decided to say nothing to Joe or Rose about Miranda, about what she knows. Before she left Seattle, she checked the adoption registry and put new ads in the paper:

```
I'm searching for my half-brother who was
born in Goa in March, 1966. Mother's name:
Iris Mason; father's name: Danny Gomez.
```

She doesn't know if this is legal or not, if they could both sue her. But they'll have to come out of hiding to do it.

At home, she finds a stack of forwarded mail and her jumbled possessions, still unpacked, in the middle of the living room. Right after she left Eddie, she went out of town on a job for five weeks. Then Elaine's death. She sets up her bed and unpacks a few things. Listens to her messages: Eddie, two girlfriends, a bar buddy wondering where she has been, the college union rep with an update on her suspension, a gig offer on a cruise to the Caribbean over Christmas and New Year's, and a cryptic message — "It's Mr. Johnstone, about your mother. Call me." — with a Winthrop telephone number. She calls the number immediately but gets no answer.

Next, she plugs in the laptop and checks e-mail. Leonard, a friend and the CEO of a firm that hired her as a consultant four years ago, has a job proposal: "The project involves a search for the Underground Railroad, an escape route used by slaves during the 19th century. There are a number of documented sites already. Hidden tunnels, shafts, shelters, back roads and forests. Does it sound interesting to you? Are you available and, if so, how soon can you come to Ohio?" He's attached a detailed file.

The project does interest her. Leonard knows her obsession with disappearing peoples. In this case, the disappearance *saved* the forty thousand slaves who used the Ohio escape route.

She *could* simply forget everything and get on with her life. Phone the lawyer up north and start the Presumed Dead proceedings. Take Leonard's offer and go to Ohio for a few months. Do the Caribbean cruise at Christmas. By then, everything would be in order: Ray back in Mexico, Elaine's possessions dealt with, Patti's murderer in jail, Iris and Kate's half-brother lost or forgotten. It'd be easier than all these excavations, all these land mines.

Of course, she doesn't forget everything. In fact, she scours directories on the web, looking for "Danny Gomez." Checks world directories. No Danny Gomez or Iris Mason. In Washington State, she finds Gomezes everywhere. Frustrated, she prints out lists of them. There are sixteen in Moses Lake alone. She'll start there. She spends a couple of hours clicking through Goa-net, as if she expects to see Iris and Danny at a Goa-trance music party at The Paraiso de Anjuna, with its "view on the sea, trance Goa DJs, and nice psychedelic decoration …," seated, perhaps, in the "dark room reserved for bad trips" or dancing "where the parties are very chaotic because of the interdictions." She checks travel sites as if she expects to find Iris and Danny sipping wine in the Banyan Tree Restaurant, or lying poolside at the Hotel Coqueiral, in green iridescent bathing suits.

She changes her clothes and repacks her suitcase, calls the girlfriends and explains that she'll be away for a while. Tries Mr. Johnstone again, but gets no answer. Then she settles in to phone the sixteen Gomezes in Moses Lake. She says, "I'm looking for a Danny Gomez who worked at Grand Coulee Dam and who would be about fifty."

After eight calls, a man says, "Yes, that would be our son. Who is this?"

"Did he live in Goa for a year?" she asks, to be sure.

"Oh ... that would have been ... a long time ago. Just a minute," he says, covering the mouthpiece. She hears him say, "It's about Danny. Somebody asking about him." Then he speaks to her again. "Here," he says. "Talk to my wife."

An elderly woman's voice. "Who's this? Why are you calling about Danny?"

Kate explains that she's trying to locate her mother, and that Danny was her friend. "Does he live in Moses Lake?" she asks.

She listens to the hollow of the telephone line for a moment. "I'm afraid we can't help you," the woman says, her voice heavy with sorrow. "Our son passed away years ago."

"I'm sorry," Kate says. "I didn't know."

"What did you say your name was?" Mrs. Gomez says. "How did you know our Danny?"

"I didn't know him." Kate explains again about her mother, ending with, "Did he leave a family behind?" She wonders if he told them about Iris, about their baby.

"Never married. Our only son, too." Mrs. Gomez sighs.

For a second, Kate wants to tell her about the baby, the possibility of continuation, survival of their family line. But she can't seed this hope without proof. She thanks her and hangs up. From her purse, she takes the packet of photos Miranda gave her. Sorts through them until she finds one with Iris and Danny — their hands interlocked, their eyes glossy with love. Melancholy overwhelms her. Love is a luminous sphere, she thinks. Two people can move in and out of its orbit so quickly.

It's now 2:30, too late to start out for Twisp. She continues to unpack, screws together the Ikea bookcases and pushes them against a wall. She opens the boxes of books and knick-knacks and puts everything on the shelves: the black wrought-iron rooster bookends Joe gave her when she was twelve; her electric kiddie-stapler — green, red and yellow plastic, moving parts under clear Plexiglass; three shards found on the Guatemalan dig; a delicate blue vase Stephen bought her the spring they went to Venice; two tiny brass frames encircling a photo of her and Angie inside a cliff dwelling of the Anasazi; and a photo of Rose embracing her at Kate's high school graduation. She empties the rest of the garbage bags and sorts everything onto the shelves, even though she hasn't washed them.

She reassembles the night table and plugs in her lamp, a limestone carving of a young woman metamorphosing into a sea creature. She's the mistress of the underworld, Sedna, who refuses suitors and marries a bird. The girl's father kills her husband and takes his daughter home in a boat. On the way, a storm arises and the father throws Sedna overboard. She clings to the boat and he chops off her fingers. These become four life forms — fish, seals, walruses and whales. Her animal children eat up her father. Sedna becomes the chief deity of the lower world, and each autumn the Inuit hold a great feast in her honour. In legends, all the scores are evened.

She eats out at Oh Darling!, a Japanese restaurant on Granville Street. Sits in a booth and reads the file Leonard sent about the new project — an excavation of tunnels and hidden rooms under the floorboards of farms and houses. What interests her even more than the physical discovery are the people who would have used the escape route. She wonders how many diaries, journals, there might be; where these people settled; how extensive their oral history is; how many of those forty thousand men and women survived. In the end, she decides to tell Leonard she's interested but not available for another month. She resists the urge to spend the night in a bar; she wants to be on the road early in the morning.

She takes the stack of mail to bed with her and sorts through it quickly. Among the bills, magazines and flyers, she finds a letter postmarked Twisp, her name and address scrawled in a shaky, unfamiliar handwriting.

Dear Kate,

We need to talk now. I have just discovered some important information about your mother. Phone me between 1:00 and 3:00 in the afternoon. We can meet in Seattle or wherever you want. Your dad has the letters. I'm sorry about everything.

Elaine

The envelope is dated the day of Elaine's death. Kate shivers, the hair at her nape bristling.

She phones her father, asks him about the note and the letters.

He hesitates, and she wishes she could see his face, read his eyes. "She must have wanted to tell you Iris was her sister ... I don't know ... the letters? I gave you those ...."

"Why didn't she phone?" Kate says, exasperated.

He sighs. "I don't know."

"I still thinks it's strange," Kate says, shaking her head, although he can't see her.

"Kate, I'm glad you called," her father says, quickly, his voice tense. "There's been new developments ... thing is ... we found Angie's fingerprints on the rug Patti was buried in. And now Angie's gone."

"What do you mean gone?"

"Gone," he says. "The diner's deserted. The baby's with a social worker. And Angie's *gone*."

"But that's crazy," Kate says. Nothing makes sense any more. "You don't think Angie killed Patti?"

"No ... no, of course not —"

"Trevor —"

"Only Angie's prints are on the rug," he says.

After she hangs up, Kate takes an Ativan to slow her breathing and dreams of disappearing herself. Like underwater swimming, she could surface for air now and again, always in a different location, unexpected and free. "Dream on," she says aloud.

She sits up and retrieves Elaine's letter from the floor. She rereads the words several times, imagining how she would have felt receiving this, were Elaine still alive. Would she have gone to meet her? She concentrates on the words *I'm sorry*. She thinks about Elaine writing out this note, posting it, maybe moments before she plunged into the river. Did Elaine really think those words would act as a salve, an exorcizing of guilt? *Guilt*. Odourless, tasteless. It sounds light, golden, *gilt-edged*, but is an over-sized suitcase inside the body. *Guilt* complex. Mother, father, husband, lover. *Guilt* trip. Invisible, everpresent, it transports people through memory along a sharp thin wire. If she could right all her wrongs, would she begin with all the things she *did* or *didn't* do? She looks back down at the words. *Your dad has the letters*. She sighs. *Thanks a lot, Elaine*.

Resurrections

August 22, 1997 / *Spirit of Discovery*

THE TASADAY

"Imagine, if you will, in the second half of the twentieth century, the discovery of a Filipino people who live in caves and still use stone tools.

"It's 1971. While elsewhere in the world the microprocessor and CAT scanning were being introduced, while the NASA *Mariner 9* became the first spacecraft to orbit another planet, President Ferdinand Marcos and Manuel Elizalde, Jr. introduced the world to the Tasaday — a tiny group of peace-loving, Stone-Age food gatherers, isolated hundreds of years in a Philippine rainforest. The discovery was hailed by some scholars as the most significant anthropological event of the twentieth century.

"Elizalde, the head of PANAMIN, a Filipino government agency for the protection of minority groups, claimed he had learned of the Tasaday through a member of a neighbouring tribe who had met them years before while hunting, and who had been trading bits of cloth and metal with them, in exchange for the Tasaday's help in watching his traps.

"Before their meeting with Elizalde, the Tasaday had had no contact with Westerners. They wore clothes made of orchid leaves, used stone tools and ate what they could gather in the rainforest: yam-like roots, fruits, nuts, small fish, crabs and tadpoles from the forest streams. They numbered seven men, six women and fourteen children.

"Although Elizalde cautioned that scientific studies should not jeopardize the Tasaday's long-sheltered lifestyle, an international media carnival ensued: anthropologists flew in and, based on a few hours of observation, concluded that the Tasaday were a real people who had been isolated geographically and culturally for around a thousand years; a *National Geographic* crew immediately filmed a documentary, *The Last Tribes of Mindanao*. During the crest of publicity in 1972, President Marcos declared about nineteen thousand hectares of land reserved for the Tasaday.

"In 1974, media contact ceased due to Marcos' imposition of martial law. Visitors were prohibited from entering the Tasaday reservation without a special permit. For the next twelve years, nothing more was heard of the tribe.

"When Marcos was ousted in 1986, the Tasaday story re-emerged. A Swiss anthropologist, Oswald Iten, had hiked to the Tasaday caves and found them deserted. The Tasaday themselves were living in huts, wearing jeans and jewellery; they were growing crops and hunting with modern weapons.

"Iten immediately pronounced the Tasaday a hoax, and claimed that the local Tboli and Manobo peoples had been coerced by Elizalde to pose as Tasaday in exchange for land and money, and that Elizalde had received fifty thousand dollars for the filming of the tribe. Had Elizalde and Marcos conceived the scheme to gain access to rainforest lands and to the valuable mahogany? There would have been no need to do this, some said: with only twenty-seven Tasaday members, the tribe could easily have been disposed of, especially during the corrupt Marcos government.

"Speculation abounded. Scientists reviewed the original documentation to prove or disprove the hoax theory, but were unable to conclusively decide either way. They all agreed the research done in 1971 was sketchy, and that the Tasaday, fifteen years later, could not be studied in the same way. They now had contact with the outside world, and were integrated into neighbouring tribes.

"Elizalde could not be questioned about the charges because he had fled to Costa Rica, and taken with him millions from the treasury of PANAMIN, bankrupting the organization.

"Is the Tasaday story a hoax? To date, numerous conferences have been held worldwide to debate the issue.

GENNI GUNN

The controversy continues and anthropologists argue both for and against the Tasaday's authenticity. What is true, however, is that whatever their name, the indigenous people involved are real, as was their exploitation."

A ll the way back to Twisp, Kate is haunted by Elaine's letter. *Nineteen years and when she finally decides to talk* ... or did Joe coerce her into a masquerade? *Distortions.*

At Marblemount, she swerves into the parking lot of the LAST TAVERN FOR 89 MILES and orders a scotch. From the roof of the tavern hang several dozen antlers — a grave roof, she thinks, wondering what happened to the bodies, hoping she's not staring at trophies. Angie has often told her that urbanites don't understand real survival. They haven't had to dig themselves out of a snowstorm, unearth a woodpile, or shoot an animal to eat through the winter. Kate has tried to explain that there are numerous deprivations possible, even in a city. How long you hold out is what counts. *Well, Elaine, you held out too long.*

Back on the highway, she climbs, descends, awed by the jutting peaks that form an imposing boundary. On the other side, in the Methow Valley, her father waits.

She slows as she approaches Angie's abandoned diner, its neon blazing like a lighthouse beacon. In the parking lot, the pipes and trenches are gone. What remains is a maze of paths — rich brown dirt against grey gravel. Beside the diner, the trailer slumps on its concrete foundation, gloomy and empty. She imagines Patti's face in the window, the baby crying. Sees, instead, the crane and tractors that whine like injured monsters in one corner of the lot. She drives on, disoriented, wondering about Angie. Where is she now? *Friendship.* An ocean liner transporting them to happier days. Friend*ship.* A luxury cruise along bittersweet memories.

She imagines Angie with her in a city bar, miniskirted, gelled and lipsticked, tipsy and laughing. She imagines Angie with her in her near-empty apartment, cross-legged on the floor, dressing gowns, no makeup, three gallons of coffee and the entire Iris story, a whirligig around them, like a runaway ghost. Angie would have been eleven when Iris came back from Goa.

She imagines what it would have been like to grow up with a younger brother. She wonders who will take Patti's baby now.

Kate thought about having a baby with Ray. She thought about it in an angel-wings, soft-focus, sugarcane, love-child kind of way, when the real hyphenation should have been Kate-Ray. They had gone down to Moses Lake for the weekend, checked into a motel overlooking the lake. It was hot in that unbearable hundred-degree heat of July. They rented a pedal boat and meandered around the shoreline, trailing their hands in the water. They had been dancing around the baby-making topic. He'd already done that, she hadn't.

"What does it matter?" Ray insisted. "The human race will not become extinct if you do not reproduce."

She started telling him about the dodo bird, weaving a sad, sentimental tale about these large docile birds that had forgotten how to fly. "Lost their ability to fly, you mean," Ray said. She continued. On the island of Mauritius, where the dodo lived, there were no mammals, so the dodo had no fear of predators. They nested on the ground and ate fruit that fell from trees. "They should have known better," Ray said. She ignored this, too. In 1505, she told him, the Portuguese landed on the island and had themselves a feast. Imagine waddling fifty-pound birds that had no fear. The Portuguese brought with them pigs and monkeys and rats that ate dodo eggs in the ground nests. Within a hundred years of the arrival of humans on the island, the dodo was rare, extinct by 1681. "To be trusting is to allow oneself to be easily betrayed," she concluded.

Ray scoffed. "The dodo was a stupid bird. That's why we call stupid people dodo-brains."

They had a terrible fight. She thinks they both knew it was because the heat was oppressive and they were stranded on water inside a pedal boat, arguing not about the dodo, but about the fact that she wanted to get pregnant and Ray didn't want another child.

She is settling back into her father's house when a woman walks slowly down the gravel road toward the door. Kate watches her approach, thinking she must have left her car up by the main road, she must be lost. The woman is wearing torn black leggings and a long sweater — magenta flowers against a faded grey background, yellow rubber boots, ski mittens. She's in her mid-fifties, older perhaps, her face a grid of lines like an inner-city map, her eyes crammed into bluish sockets, her tight-permed hair frosted silver. She's carrying a clear-plastic purse jammed full.

Kate wipes her hands and goes to open the door before the woman knocks.

They stare at each other for a moment. Up close, the woman has the gaunt look of a burnout. "May I help you?" Kate says.

"I'm who you're looking for," the woman says, slips off the mittens and holds out her hand for Kate to shake.

No. She frowns. "You're?"

"Your mother," the woman says, matter-of-fact. She takes Kate's hand and shakes it. "Well? Aren't you going to ask me in?"

Kate steps aside. Her throat burns, her thoughts fracas through her brain. She's unprepared. She swallows several times while the woman walks through the kitchen to the living room, as if she knows the way. Kate follows her, bewildered by her feelings, which border on repulsion.

The woman sits in Joe's chair and puts her purse and mittens on her lap. Kate concentrates on the plastic, on the floating cosmetics — lipstick, powder-puff, eye and lip pencils — scrunched Kleenex, bits of paper, folded coupons, nail clippers, scissors and three bottles of purple nail polish. Tries to stop the trembling of her hands.

"So," the woman says, as if this were a complete sentence.

"Are you sure?" Kate says softly, so as not to insult her.

The woman looks at her sternly. "Of course I'm sure. You wanted to find me. Well, here I am." She opens her purse and fishes inside until she finds a newspaper clipping she hands Kate.

Kate opens it and reads. It's one of the ads she placed in the newspapers. She stares at it for a few moments, trying to compose her thoughts. She had expected she'd have time to prepare before she met her mother, that she'd be able to choose questions to ask her, that their reunion would be joyous and emotional. It reminds her of that summer when Iris came back from Goa to live with them, that summer when Kate was neither happy nor sad as much as she was careful. She watched her mother's every movement and kept her in sight. There were no extravagant emotional displays, no mother/daughter scenes in yellow meadows. Her great anxiety stemmed from the fact that she had to accept that Iris was back when she could, at any moment, disappear.

She looks up at this woman, her mother who isn't the

mother she imagined at all, neither demon nor angel, but rather a pitiful creature. "Why didn't you ever contact me?" she says, surprised at the anger in her voice.

The mother-Kate-doesn't-want sighs. "It was so long ago, and I was so young then .... We all make mistakes," her mother says, and looks to Kate for approval, under heavy, hooded lids. "I didn't know where to find you."

"That's bullshit!" Kate shouts and gets up. "Why did you come if you can't even be honest?" She begins to pace, her arms crossed tight against her body.

Her mother's shoulders hunch and her head hangs down. Kate should feel pity. Instead, her rage increases. Thirty years of resentment is not going to dissipate. "You were too busy fucking. Why don't you say that? It would be closer to the truth."

The mother-Kate-doesn't-want begins to cry, soft, soundless. Kate bites her lip, not wanting to feel any sympathy for her. She has so many questions to ask, but this feels all wrong. She had imagined them together, lying across the bed upstairs, talking in undertones. She had imagined Iris would ask about her life so far, would tell Kate the exquisite details of her own childhood, of her love for Joe, for Danny, of her betrayals. She stares at her mother, at her heaving shoulders, stares while Iris opens the plastic purse and takes out a rumpled Kleenex and wipes her eyes. Despite herself, Kate wants to go to her, put her arms around her, forgive her. Instead, she says, "What happened to the other baby?"

She looks up at Kate, stunned. "What baby?"

"When you came back from Goa. Danny Gomez' baby. What did you do with him?"

"I don't know anything about the baby," Iris says, and straightens. She pats her hair at her temples several times, obviously agitated. Then she reaches across, clasps Kate's arm and pulls her closer. "He made me do it," she whispers. "I didn't want to give up the baby. Honest, I didn't." She lets go and starts crying again.

"Where is the baby now?" Kate says, exasperated, but her mother doesn't answer.

Kate leaves her crying and goes into the kitchen to pour herself a scotch. Of all the scenarios she has dreamed up, she never once thought her mother could be crazy. It makes sense, though, when she thinks about the stories. Perhaps Iris has been in a psychiatric hospital all these years. Maybe Joe put her there and didn't want Kate to know. She pours her mother a drink, too, and carries it into the living room. Iris has stopped crying and is sitting with her hands on her lap.

"Here, drink this," Kate says.

Iris takes it and sips, then sets the glass on the coffee table. "I'm sorry," she says.

Kate sighs deeply. "It's OK." She pats Iris' arm and sits on the couch.

Iris looks at her longingly. "You're so grown up," she says. "I feel cheated I wasn't there to watch it happen." She sits with her back straight, her legs together, her yellow rubber boots crossed at the ankles, her hands folded in her lap. Even with the mittens and purse and torn leggings, she looks dignified, serene.

"You chose that," Kate says, her voice brittle.

"Was made to," she corrects, then leans forward, picks up the glass and takes a long drink.

Kate puts her glass down. Outside, her father's car inches up the drive. Her mother, Iris — she doesn't know what to call her — gets up as soon as she sees him. "He mustn't find me here," she says. "He won't like it one bit." She looks at Kate, terrified.

Kate puts her arm around her. "It's all right," she says.

"No, you don't understand. Oh ...." Her mother leans into Kate, only there are no tears. Her arm slides around Kate's waist, her fingers dig into Kate's ribs. She holds the plastic purse tight against her chest, like a shield.

The door opens and closes. Joe calls out Kate's name.

"In here," Kate says. "We have a visitor." She takes a deep breath.

Joe stands in the doorway and stares at them for a moment, puzzled, annoyed. Then he sighs deeply. "Hello, Betsy," he says. "So this is where you've got to." He crosses the room and detaches the woman from Kate, like one might do with a monkey, one limb at a time. Betsy puts up no resistance. "Everyone's been worried about you," Joe says, in a voice normally used for children. "Poor Jack's been out looking for you all afternoon."

"Who is she?" Kate half whispers.

Joe taps his temple a couple of times, over Betsy's head. "Lives up in town. She's been missing all day." He reaches for the phone. "I better call her husband," he says.

Kate falls into a chair, her chest as tight as if someone were sitting on it, ping-ponging between relief and disappointment. Betsy's eyes plead with her to take her away from Joe; they say she's afraid of him. Perhaps he's returned her to her home too often. Yet he holds her very intimately, gently. Now and then, even as he explains to her husband that she's fine, he leans into Betsy and says, "It's all right, really," his voice soothing, the same voice Kate imagines he must have used with Iris after all those crazy episodes. It makes Kate think that her mother might be just like this woman, and she's not sure she wants to know that.

Long after Joe has left with Betsy, Kate sits in the living room, stunned, analyzing her feelings. *I* should not be searching for Iris, she thinks. It should be *her* looking for me. Iris clearly doesn't want to be found and maybe Kate has no right to pry open what her mother has slammed shut. She goes upstairs, takes out her notebook and rereads everything. She checks off what she has examined. There's not much left: the rest of the trunk contents, the saddle.

In the first trunk, a paper trail: travel brochures to tropical countries — St. Lucia, Jamaica, Nigeria, Brazil; glossy photos of teenagers strolling hand in hand on white sand, the sea an impossible aquamarine; palms lined up like chorus girls, their feather headdresses swaying; young couples in Tilley shorts and hats, kissing against a LandRover; the yellow spotted necks of giraffes; lovers rowing down the Amazon, the jungle thicket both wild and tamed to safety in the photo. A handful of sheet music to Joan Baez songs, chords written above the bars in pen: "Let Your Love Flow," "No Woman No Cry," "Daddy You Been On My Mind," "It's All Over Now," "Baby Blue." A copy of Dr. Spock's *Baby and Child Care*, with an inscription from Rose. An envelope of newspaper clippings about Judy Collins and Marianne Faithful. A lipstick imprint on a yellowed Kleenex. A road map of Goa, villages circled in green.

She returns everything to the steamer trunk, closes it and carries it out to the shed. Then she brings in the second trunk. She has to break this lock too. It's an old-fashioned hope chest crammed with embroidered tablecloths, crocheted doilies, appliquéd pillowcases, linen dish towels and, at the very bottom, three tiny newborn outfits. She takes them out slowly, unfolds them. One looks like a christening gown — long, off-white satin, with smocked bodice. Did Iris sew this? She holds it up to her face, smells the fabric, wondering if it belongs to her or to the other baby, when something floats out of its sleeve. She picks up the photo from the floor and stares at the black-and-white baby face, trying to decipher it, to read her own features, but the baby looks too generic, too young to have acquired distinct characteristics. She puts everything back in this trunk too, everything except the photo, which she slips into her wallet. Then she replaces the trunk in the shed.

She lies down on the bed and thinks about her mother, her unhappy life in the five years she spent here, on and off, not so unlike Kate's own life. She wishes she'd known her grandparents. She wishes she and Elaine had trusted each other. *Dear Iris, what are you running from?*

When she tries to think about Iris returning from Goa, abandoned, when she tries to think about what could have happened to the baby Iris must have brought to this house — *Get that bastard baby out of this house!* — the bundle inside the shawl, the graveyard, when she tries to think about all this, she can't believe how little she knows. How is it that parents can operate in complete secrecy around their children, their faces like masks the Mayans put over the dead?

Finally she goes downstairs and begins to cook supper, planning her next move. She'll go home. She'll take Elaine's quilt, the trunks, Iris's clothes. The sewing boxes, no. She fills her mind with physical objects, subtracting their meaning. It's easier than wondering what will happen to her and Joe. Easier than wondering who Iris is. Easier than wondering whether she and Angie can ever be the friends they once were. Easier than thinking about Ray, to face the dread that she won't see him again. But it was *she* who abandoned *him*, of course, for reasons that now escape her.

Over supper, Joe tells her about Betsy: she had an abortion many years ago and never recovered, mentally. Now she imagines a child somewhere is looking for her. She answers all the ads, trying to squeeze herself into the lives of strangers.

"She implied her husband made her do it," Kate says, watching him carefully.

"Who knows?" He shrugs.

"Can nothing be done for her?" Kate asks.

"She's harmless, really." He picks up the plates and gets up. "I suppose they could put her on some tranquilizer or other, but what's the point? Jack — her husband — has no problem looking after her. Sometimes she wanders off ... but she can't go far."

Kate remains seated while he hovers around her, stacks dishes, fills the sink. Finally she says, "Was Iris a bit crazy too? Like Betsy, I mean?"

"No!" he says, emphatically. "She was not like Betsy at all." Then he clams up.

Kate gets up and makes coffee though it's evening, and it'll probably keep her up half the night. She figures she'll temper it with a good dose of scotch. "She did some pretty weird stuff," she insists. "Rose told me about the blue thread."

Joe pulls his hand out of the sink and clasps it, wet, on her forearm. "Your mother," he says firmly, "might have been what they'd now call manic-depressive. She had times when she was up, and times when she was so blue she could hardly get out of bed. But she was never crazy. Do you understand?" His eyes bore into Kate's, daring her to contradict him. His hand is still curled around her arm, squeezing.

She shrugs off his hand. "I thought she spent time in some psychiatric hospital. That's what I remember." She moves away from him then, fills the Bodum with water and balances the plunger on top of it.

"Iris was gentle, innocent in her own way," he says. "She did things without thinking, impulsively. What seemed crazy to other people, made sense to her." He stares into space for a moment. "She was very distraught. She went away to rest. But you were too small to remember."

Snow. Christmas morning 1966, the year Iris returned from Goa. And there Kate is in her room, a three-year-old in Donald Duck pajamas, four Raggedy Ann dolls lined up with their heads on her pillow, their button eyes everopen. Something has awakened her, a dog's bark, perhaps, or an avalanche of snow gliding off the roof. Outside, a blizzard so dense, her window resembles a black-and-white TV tuned to static. Snow has accumulated in triangles at the edges of the panes, has turned the window into a Christmas card.

Kate gets out of bed, straightens the gingham dresses and wooly pigtails of the dolls, then pulls up the blanket to cover their freckled faces. She wonders if Santa has come. Perhaps that's what woke her: Santa struggling back up the chimney, or one of his reindeer pawing the snow. There may be new dolls downstairs, or a set of miniature cups and saucers — pale blue with yellow daisies — or a dollhouse, a pink cross-section, one wall missing, filled with tiny wooden chairs and beds and dressers. She pulls on a big sweater and tiptoes downstairs.

The tree lights flash on and off, bathing the room in red, green, white. Kate sits under the tree and stares at the wrapped gifts. She keeps very still because she doesn't want Mummy to wake up. She's a little afraid of Mummy, who cries all the time now. Kate doesn't know what she did wrong. She concentrates on the pretty ribbons under the tree, smoothes out the curly ones, then lets them spring back into coiled streamers. After a few minutes, she hears footsteps, and freezes, trying to make herself invisible. Then Daddy's whisper, *Iris?*

Kate shrinks farther under the tree and waits for him to come into the room. She hopes he won't be angry. He's in his pajamas too, and his hair is sticking up on one side. He smiles when he sees her. *Merry Christmas, Pumpkin.* He picks her up and ruffles her hair. *I see Santa's been here.* He smells musky. Kate lays her head on his shoulder and sucks her thumb. *Have you seen Mummy?* She shakes her head. *We'd better go find her, then.* He carries her around the house as they search, making a game of it. Then, Daddy sets her down next to the Christmas tree. *Wait here.* Kate hears him put on his boots and coat and go out.

She gets up, pulls on her boots and goes out too. The snow has drifted onto the porch and collected on the steps. She follows her father, her feet in his footprints along the pearly driveway. The footsteps turn into the orchard, spread farther and farther apart. Kate plows through the snow, her pajamas cold and wet and clinging to her legs.

Oh my God! Kate looks up, alarmed. He's carrying Mummy in his arms, like Kate carries her baby doll. He's running toward Kate. *Get inside. Now!*

Iris' head is limp over Joe's arm, her hair frosted and icy, her wrists red, caked with sludgy liquid. *Hold on, Iris.* Joe clutches her so tightly his shirt is a widening red stain. Kate is terrified by them both. She turns and flees through the snow, wet and panting, her father calling after her, *Kate! Come inside. Now!* She continues to run, following his footsteps until she falls into a dark hole, packed red snow.

She remembers shrieking. She remembers a neighbour trying to soothe her as Joe and Iris drove away. She remembers waiting an eternity until her father returned. Iris came home months later, in early spring.

She takes two souvenir mugs out of the cupboard — I ❤ Italy, La$ Vega$ — and puts them on the table. Has he visited these places? *Artifacts. Traces.* She knows nothing about him. *Incriminations.* She must remove everything that belongs to her, clear this house of her presence, of the past and its ghosts, disappear. She fills the mugs with coffee and sets them down, her hand unsteady.

Joe does not notice. He rinses the last plate and sets it in the rack. After he fishes the plug out of the drain and dries his hands on a dishcloth, he takes his mug and goes into the living room. Kate hears the springs of his favourite chair, the click of the light switch, the rustle of newspaper.

She takes her coffee upstairs, opens her suitcase and begins to throw things in. She clears the room in a frenzy: shoes, clothes, purses, tissues, books, glass, mug ... from the bathroom, she removes soap, makeup, toothbrush, toothpaste, floss, shampoo, conditioner, bath towel, face cloth. Then she wipes everything down. But, of course, it's useless. *Every contact leaves a trace.* She scrubs down the walls, the table, the bed .... *Whenever any two objects come into contact with one another, they affect one another in some way* ... the chair, the closet, the door, the mirror. *This is madness,* she thinks, dropping the cloth. She stares at her hands: even here, the trace of her sewing, her fingers full of tiny puncture marks, indelible reminders, blood memories.

She lies down, wraps the quilt around herself and, for a moment, the triangles, squares and blocks fuse into Iris, her arms, her hands encircling Kate. Cat's cradle .... *When the bow breaks, the cradle will fall* .... She wonders what sadist would sing that to children .... *And down will come baby* ... a newspaper clipping, a front-page photo of Iris standing on the Capilano Suspension Bridge, peering over the edge into the two-hundred-and-thirty-foot drop below. Her face is calm, as if she were looking at a deer grazing by the riverbank, or a particularly brilliant patch of wildflowers. What you won't see in the photo is that down below, a baby lies face down, cradled in leaves — her fall broken by the expansive arms of firs.

The room feels dank and cold. Kate shivers and listens. Not a sound. It's only a quarter to ten, but her father must have gone to bed already. She gets up, tiptoes downstairs and escapes into the crisp night air. Drives to Winthrop, straight to The Palace, sits at the high bar across from the stage, orders a scotch. Matt's sitting at a table. He nods when he sees her. It's a new band, near the end of its first set. Kate drinks her scotch quickly, feels the heat burn a welcome swath all the way down, soothing her restlessness. She's waving her hand to order another when Matt smiles. He snaps his fingers, nods in her direction, and the waitress brings him their drinks.

"So. You're back," he says, setting the scotch in front of her.

She shrugs, elbows on the bar counter. The band is playing a garage-version of "Stormy Monday," guitar player leaned back and wailing in endless solos. It's impossible to speak above it, so they listen to one stormy day after the other.

"I'm not hitting on you," Matt says, when they can hear each other.

"Yeah?" Kate sips her scotch, then looks at him, eyes unwavering.

He smiles.

She shakes her head, decides to leave it alone. They stare at the couples who have wandered onto the dance floor, like bees attracted by salad dressing.

"You want to dance?" He stands and touches her elbow.

They walk onto the floor and begin to move their feet back and forth in time to the music. His arm tightens around her waist and she closes her eyes, falls through time and space until she's fifteen again and they're in the back seat of his dad's car. He's whispering about their elopement, as he has for months now, a ritual that elevates their back-seat sex into *Endless Love*. She is eighteen, twenty, twenty-five, thirty; she is then, now, always, her mother's daughter.

It takes her a few seconds to register Matt's erection pressing against her pelvis. She feels her chest constrict and she is overcome with exhaustion, as if she were breathing toxic air.

Bodycheck, bodyguard, body language. Mother tongue.

"Don't," she says, looking up at him.

He executes a turn, pulls her closer, avoids her eyes. "Lighten up," he says in a breezy, confident tone.

Kate pushes again, this time butting him with her elbows.

He yokes her tighter, despite her arms between them, grinds his erection into her.

She slaps him, hard across the face. Matt is too stunned to do anything but touch his cheek. Kate turns and walks off the dance floor, her shoulders squared, calm and composed until she gets in her car, where her arms and legs shake.

The cabin is completely dark when she arrives three-quarters of an hour later. It's after midnight. She gets out of the car, rushes up the steps and knocks repeatedly.

The whole way here, all she's been able to think about is Ray. Their time together is a series of short takes she has rewound and replayed until she has memorized all the words, the gestures, until she can laugh and cry in the right places. Fast-forward through the absences and you have a relation*ship* — yet another way to traverse the frozen lake of the heart, the ninety-six percent liquid of our bodies.

She continues to bang on the door until she sees his bedroom light switch on. Then, a silhouette across the room, the porch light. She moves aside, impatient.

Ray opens the door a couple of inches, sees her and opens it wider. "Kate. What's the matter?" He frowns, his eyes blinking with sleep, his hair dishevelled. It suddenly occurs to her that he could have a woman inside. "Has something happened?" he says, rubbing his hand over his collarbone.

"I'm sorry. I'm sorry." She turns to go back down the stairs. "I never should have come." She steps back, but Ray takes her arm.

He opens the door wider and pulls her in. He's wearing only his jeans. She stands inside the door while he goes back to his bedroom to get a T-shirt. She crosses her arms, hugs herself. He leaves the bedroom door open so that an oblong of gold falls into the living room.

The Rivera-like murals are gone. In their place, a disturbing black-and-white one, a series of thick black jagged edges, as if shaped by uneven pinking shears. The mural incorporates the ceiling, so that the room itself resembles the night sky. There is a geyser whose spurt holds up the world. Below this, a lake filled with humans, monsters. Then the mural's focus: from floor to ceiling, a black hole.

EVENT HORIZON: the surface of a black hole, the boundary at which the escape velocity equals the speed of light and beyond which nothing can escape.

Kate stares in the semi-darkness, afraid she will be sucked into its gravitational field, turned into a singularity — a distortion of time and space.

She turns away and sees Ray emerge from the bedroom in technicolour, his hands tucking the T-shirt into his jeans.

"A black hole," she says and points at it.

He stares at the wall, then at her. "You been drinking?" he asks, finally.

She shakes her head, even though she has, but it's not the kind of drinking he means.

"I'll make you a coffee," he says, fingers combing his hair. He walks toward the kitchen.

"What is it?" she asks.

He turns and looks at the mural as if he's only just noticed it. "Autopsy report," he says and shrugs.

She frowns, shakes her head, and he points to a piece of paper on a table. Then he goes to make the coffee.

She picks up the paper. On the top right-hand corner, the words: PATTI KONSTANTIN. AUTOPOSY NO. TW-54-97. On the bottom half of the page are the drawings of two skulls facing each other in profile, and in the upper half, a cross-section of the skull. The black hole corresponds to the head wound indicated by a ballpoint circle. She falls back into the wicker armchair, breathless.

Ray returns with two cups and stands in the doorway, temporarily blinded. He forms a black space against the wall. Once she stood at the surface of his boundary, his heartbeat and her escape velocity almost in synch.

When his eyes adjust, he moves forward and hands her the coffee, leans against the mural so that he becomes one of the chiaroscuros. She tells him about Iris' newborn, Betsy, her mother's suicide attempt. She tells him everything except what she came here to say.

He listens without interrupting, his presence intimate, his silence distant.

"What about Patti's baby?" she says. "What will happen to her?"

"I'm taking her," Ray says. "I've already seen a lawyer and started the paperwork. I don't think Trevor will fight it."

She sighs, thinking for one brief hysterical moment,

We could do it together. Instead, she tells him what she has never told anyone, that years ago she went to the SPCA and adopted a small black kitten with yellow eyes and white booties. It was barely weaned, almost blind. When she got it home, it trembled and mewed pitifully. The only thing that calmed it was to lie on her chest, against her heart. For weeks, she fretted over it, played with it, coaxed it until it trusted her completely. She and Stephen had recently parted; it was February, cold, miserable. One Friday night she was out with a girlfriend and they decided, on a whim, to drive down to Seattle to see a band. One thing led to another, Seattle became Portland, Portland became San Francisco. When she got back a week later, the kitten was dead on her pillow.

"How could I do that?" she says. "I must be a monster." She can hear their breath in the air. She speaks quickly, without looking at him. "Ray, I know I've been a monster —"

"Kate, don't," he says so firmly she chokes back the rest.

Ray embraces her and she cries against him while he holds her stiffly. There's no turning back, not really, the past an expanding universe. There's only moving ahead, reinventing herself.

The house is blazing with light, Angie's car in the drive. Kate takes a deep breath and climbs the stairs. In the kitchen, she finds Joe in his robe, his arms around Angie, who is crying. They both look up when she comes in.

"It's all right," Joe says and pats Angie's back.

"What's happened?" Kate asks. "Angie, what's going on?"

"I had nothing to do with Patti's death. She and Trevor had a fight that night ... but he didn't know, you see ... he said she fell back against a dresser. It was an accident. He didn't even know ... I came home that night ... the trailer was lit up, doors open, baby screaming ... I panicked ... wrapped Patti in the rug and buried her ... he's my son ... I had to do what I could ...."

"It'll be all right," Joe says again.

It'll be all right? Kate thinks. To what, exactly, is he referring? She presses her arms tight across her chest, her hands nestled in her underarms. Slowly Angie recedes to a distant place in her heart, like someone left standing at a railway station. Diminished. "You buried Patti to cover for Trevor?" she says, her voice cold and detached.

"It wasn't like that," Angie says passionately. "It was an accident."

Kate recreates a different scenario, one in which Trevor smashes Patti's head against the dresser and calmly leaves. She imagines Angie witnessing all this. Versions.

"It was an accident," Angie says again. "He didn't mean to do it."

Doubt is a malignant tumour. Once it begins to swell and spread, no recovery is possible. Kate stares at her father, watches him stroke Angie's back. How is he capable of such tenderness?

But she knows he is. She sees him through her eight-year-old eyes, in late August one year, when he took her to Seattle to buy school clothes. In the department store, the two of them walked along slippery gleaming aisles, her shoes loud and reverberating against the ceramic tiles. There were mannequins perched on pedestals, their sightless eyes gazing at distant horizons, their arms poised like mimes, elbows out, slender fingers bent. Joe held her tightly by the hand until they reached the children's section. Kate picked out several things she liked — bell-bottoms, T-shirts, a pink ribbed sweater, black tights and a green miniskirt. Joe held on to each one until Kate said she was finished. Then he found a saleslady and handed her over. Sat in a straight-back chair against a mirrored post and waited. Kate tried on the clothes, modelled them for him, and he smiled, delighted. They piled all the boxes in the trunk and went to a restaurant for supper. Joe said Kate could order whatever she wanted, but she said she'd have exactly the same as he had. He reached over and kissed her on the side of the head.

Has she really forgotten that Dad, the one who wrote her secret notes — "in invisible ink" — on banana skins, notes she'd discover only when she opened her lunch box: "*I love you, Sweetie.*" "*Daddy sends a kiss.*" The same Dad who let her go to work with him some Saturdays, let her sit behind his desk and draw pictures.

She stares at him now, trying to hear him order them

all out of the house — Iris, the baby, Kate — but all she hears is his voice soothing Angie.

They are actors in a play, their faces creased with appropriate emotions, their mouths opening and shutting. Their words float into the air and disperse, like smoke rings, edges leaching into each other, until the room is thick with overlapping vowels and consonants.

In the morning, she quickly dumps the contents of her suitcase onto the bed and repacks — this time only her own belongings. *Let Iris come and claim her own past.* She gathers all her mother's memorabilia and takes them out to the shed. She replaces everything in its original order, according to the grid she drew in her notebook, as if to neutralize an ancient curse, to mitigate the anger of the gods. When she is finished, she wipes everything down to remove her own traces.

She takes one last look upstairs, at her old room, trying to elicit childhood, something good to take away, but nothing surfaces. Before she leaves, she tries Mr. Johnstone's number one last time.

SADDLE [5]

Iris took up horseback riding the year she came home again, this time from a psychiatric hospital in Spokane. March 1967. Elaine wrote:

Your dad told me this. Iris was fragile, both physically and mentally, and your dad didn't know how to act around her. He didn't want to upset her in any way. She was home and she did what most people did, but she lacked heart, spirit.

Kate remembers this mother too: the one who made beds, cooked dinner, watched TV, but never spoke to Kate directly. Kate hovered near her, but never too close, flattened herself against walls, like a cat-burglar on a twenty-storey balcony. She adored her mother silently and carefully, made herself invisible, but her father's arms found her, picked her up. It was always his hands that curled around hers, his questions, his laughter.

In early May, Iris seemed to awaken from a deep slumber. She began to rise earlier, to join Joe and Kate for breakfast. Then she said she wanted to paint the house. Joe took them to Wenatchee to choose colours — Sandstone and Brick. When Iris had finished that, she started a sewing bee that lasted a week and had Kate outfitted for two seasons. Then in early June, Iris decided she wanted to take horseback lessons. Joe was ecstatic that Iris was "coming out of it."

Iris insisted on going to Mazama, to the Early Winters homestead — a packing outfit — and talked Joe into buying her a saddle even though he was worried that horseback riding wouldn't last any longer than her other whims. But it did. At first she went only in the afternoons.

Within a month, a couple of hours swelled to seven. Joe dropped Kate off at a neighbour's house on his way to work and picked her up on the way home.

As the days lengthened into summer then shortened into fall, they saw less and less of Iris. Kate was in bed when she returned, late at night, from one bar or another. She would have been asleep and wouldn't have heard the arguments between Iris and Joe, arguments that had begun as reproaches and silences and mushroomed into shouting matches and evacuation orders.

Kate covers her ears. Muffled argument, moans .... She is four years old, slowly walking along the upstairs hall, a wall of rough, dark logs under her palm. She stops, reaches for the doorknob and opens the door of her parents' room.

Her mother looks up, surprised, and quickly disentangles herself from the man in the bed. She slips on her dressing gown and stands between the bed and Kate, trying to shield the man. Danny. Kate hears the lighter flick, and a small flame flutters across the room. *Fugitive ghost*. Then the lighter snaps shut, and a fume of smoke swirls to the ceiling.

"I told you to stay downstairs," her mother says, her voice low, raspy.

The child Kate is wary, silent. Her mother's eyes narrow, her brow furls. She nudges Kate into the hall, shuts the bedroom door, then marches her downstairs. In the entrance, she grabs a tiny ski jacket from the hook by the door and pushes Kate's arms into the sleeves. She coaxes Kate into her snow boots, wraps a scarf around her neck and slips her string mittens around her shoulders. Finally Iris opens the front door, smacks Kate on the bum and thrusts her onto the covered porch. It's snowing. Beyond the porch, thick grey clouds shroud the orchard.

"Stay there," her mother says and slams the door.

Kate stands, uncertain, looks at the closed door, at the trees past the porch, their limbs cocooned in snow. An argument begins inside, her mother's and the man's voices raised. Kate clears off a little half moon and sits on the top step, watching the swirls in front of her. The muffled argument continues. Now and then Kate looks back at the door.

Car tires crunch on snow. Her father drives up, stops, gets out of the car. He's wearing his police uniform. The voices inside the house are loud and mixed with the thud of falling objects. Joe leans into Kate, says something she can't hear above the avalanche of words that tumble inside her head.

"As I recall, she went off with one of the packers," Mr. Johnstone says, "Gomez was his name, if I remember correctly."

Kate grips the receiver, remains motionless. Iris still wanted him, even after he abandoned her and the baby. *She still chose him over me.* She tries to will the thought away, but it grows and spreads like a tree disease. *Habituation*

refers to the reduction in the level of physiological response to a
stress situation.

"You don't remember where they went?" she says, finally.

"That's asking too much." He chuckles. "Besides, when people run away, they don't tell anyone where they're going."

"No, I suppose not," she says and pauses. "Thank you for your help. I'm afraid Mr. Gomez passed away."

"That's right! I remember reading it years ago," Mr. Johnstone says. "Shot in the face, wasn't he? Gomez was a bit of a scrapper. Didn't surprise no one."

"Yes," Mrs. Gomez says. "He was murdered. But we don't like to think about that. It's not going to bring him back."

"Can you tell me what happened?" Kate asks. She explains that her mother ran away with their son and that she'd like to know where he was living, what kind of person he was when he was killed — anything that might give her a clue as to where Iris could be now.

Mrs. Gomez sighs. "I don't know much about it, 'cause they never caught who did it." She pauses and Kate waits. "It's a terrible thing, not knowing." Kate hears the rustle of plastic, then Mrs. Gomez blows her nose. "A couple of kids were out camping and their dog ... started digging ... barking and whatnot ...."

"That's how they found his body," Kate prompts.

"Not really a body," Mrs. Gomez says. "Bones ... remains ... he was part mummified."

"Mummified?" Kate says. When Mr. Johnstone said "shot in the face," she imagined an execution-style murder, a fresh body dumped in the woods. Catastrophic event.

"It wasn't a recent murder," Mrs. Gomez says. "When they found him, ten years ago, he'd been dead a long time. About twenty years."

Kate does the math.

She gets in her car and begins to drive south, east, propelled by a memory, a small kitten at the side of a highway ... but it's her father's memory. She stops the car, turns around and races back to the house. She fishes a couple of diazepam from her purse and swallows them. Two hundred and six bones in the body ... fluvial water, an excellent preservative because of the silt and sand ... for mummification to occur, all water must be removed from the body ... *gross stress: anticipatory, impact, recoil, post-traumatic* ... a burial fixes a point in time ... Kennewick *Wo*man, found in the shallow waters of Columbia Park ... a ninety-two hundred-year-old skeleton .... In geological time, thirty years is a flutter of cicada wings.

It begins to snow the cut-outs against the window of a children's classroom at Christmas. White doilies glide onto the windshield and stick. Kate turns into their gravel road and parks right in front of the house, motor running. And suddenly it's November, 1967. She's sitting on the top step, listening to her mother and a man argue inside the house. Her father drives up. He says something, and Kate points to the house. Joe gathers her up and puts her in the front seat of the car, motor running. The snow falls in thick flat flakes that quickly cover the windows. She waits like that Inca child on the icy mountaintop. Walled in.

She turns on the windshield wipers; reaches for the door handle and it gives easily. *It's thirty years later.* She forces herself inside. Joe's not home, but she doesn't care. She goes directly to his room, slides open drawers and spills the contents onto the bed. *Your dad has the letters.* Underwear, socks, T-shirts, hankies, fraying shorts, sweatpants, lumbar support, hot-water bottle. In the drawer of the bedside table, book, pen, coins, candle, flashlight, batteries. She throws it all back, opens the closet, moves aside the hangers and takes down boxes. She sits on the floor and goes through everything. *A burial fixes a point in time. November 24th 1967.* She finds the deed to the house. A will, making her beneficiary. Clippings of letters he has written and had published in various newspapers, on various subjects. Letters from friends, business associates, Elaine. She checks the dates of these, but finds the first one dated when she was about thirteen.

Then, a wooden box découpaged with sepia photographs of Iris and Joe, their faces heartbreakingly young. She opens the box, her heart pounding. Gold charms. Green and blue plastic mermaid swizzle-sticks. The letters. She unfolds them, her hands trembling.

December 26, 1967

Dear Mummy,

I hope you had a happy Christmas. I love my bunny rabbit with the soft ears. And the jellybeans too. Today I am very happy because yesterday I had a visit from Santa Claus. He was a very jolly, fat man who had a voice a little bit like Daddy's. He brought me a baby carriage for my doll, a train and a BIG doll, almost as big as me. And I got a stocking full of chocolates, caramels and oranges and one piece of coal that Daddy said was for when I was a little bit naughty. I got everything I wanted. When you come, I'll show you everything. Write me a long letter soon and tell me how you are and when you're coming to see me, and what Santa Claus brought you. I miss you. Hurry up.

Katey

June 2, 1968

Dear Mummy,

Thank you very much for my bride doll and for the pink princess hat and the card. I remember you always. A little while ago, we ate a delicious cake because it was my birthday. Daddy and I thought about you and I wish you could have had some cake with us. I asked Daddy if I could send you a piece and he laughed and said it was not possible. We'll eat it together another time. Daddy promised to take me to the beach at Auntie Rose's house, later when it's hot. I'm having a birthday party next Saturday. Can you come please?

Katey

May 8, 1969

Dear Mummy,

Today we made Mother's Day cards at kindergarten and gifts too. When the teacher got to my desk, she looked at my card, then said I should write the card to Daddy. "But it's not Father's Day," I told her. "And anyway my mother might come this Sunday." And I hope you do, because I have a GREAT card for you, all decorated with flowers, just like your name. Daddy let me plant my very own outside and they are almost two feet tall! I hope you will come to see me soon.

Your daughter, Katey

August 12, 1969

Dear Mummy,

Thank you for your letter that I was waiting for for so long. I wish I could see you. I promise to be good and to study at school. I'll be in Grade 1 soon. I'm a little bit scared because it's the big school. Daddy won't let me have a new dress and shoes, but everybody else has them. I wish you could come to school with me and tell my teacher who you are. Daddy bought me a green lunch box and it has a thermos inside where I can put my juice. Every day I look for your letters in the mail box. Please come soon.

Your daughter, Kathleen Mason

She stares at the dates. *Hurry up.* She sees her father sitting with her on those Saturday mornings when she wrote these letters — *how do you spell "thermos"?* — letters he never sent. She listened to her father read replies from Iris, held letters in her hand, read them herself, opened the gifts Iris had chosen for her. Kate imagines Joe, long after she was asleep, composing Iris' letters. She imagines him buying gifts and wrapping them carefully. She imagines Joe fabricating the life of a woman who no longer existed. A mother's disappearance — *an event for which the adaptive infrastructure is unprepared.* How is it possible he would let her believe Iris abandoned them? She fingers the letters, the paper as brittle as the sentimental dad who kept them.

She puts on her jacket and goes outside to sit on the porch, to wait for him. The snow has long stopped, and the steps shimmer, as if coated with metallic fibre, evening wear. The thick shroud of clouds has vanished and stars begin to blink, awakened. She goes back inside and gets the quilt; winds it around herself, like a talisman.

When dusk transforms to night, she sees the lights of his Explorer jolt up the gravel road, illuminating the trees to either side, limbs now bare of apples, wrinkled leaves yellow and red and ready to fall. She concentrates on the headlights that appear like beast's eyes boring into the dark. Her father parks behind her car, gets out.

HEARTSTRINGS: rope bridges across the chasms between them.

HEARTACHE, HEARTBREAK: a shattering, shards of heart imbedded on the inside walls of the body.

HEARTLESS: failures of the heart.

"It's going to be all right," he says, as he comes toward her. "Angie and Trevor ... there'll be charges, but it was an accident and we've found a good lawyer ...." When he's at the bottom of the steps, he stops and stares at Kate, at how odd she must seem wrapped in the quilt. "What's wrong?" he says.

She holds out the letters. "Would you explain these?" she says, her voice thin and barely controlled.

In the dark, he can't see what they are. He reaches for them and walks past her, opens the door and turns on the hall light. He freezes in the doorway, his shadow elongated and extended down the stairs, a negative mirage.

"Let me explain," he says, quietly. He closes the door and their shadows blend into the night. He sits next to her on the step.

"I know about Danny Gomez," she says, to stop him from inventing whatever lie he's about to tell her. "My mother didn't leave." Her arms are crossed tight around her chest, and in her head an ice storm whirls.

He puts the letters in her lap, then leans forward on his elbows and presses his palms together in front of his mouth, as if praying.

"What I did, Kate," he says, at last, "I did for you."

"You bastard!" she says and stands up. "You bastard!"

"I was trying to protect you. That's why I didn't tell you."

"Protect me?" Her voice is shrill, unfamiliar. "Or save yourself?" She swipes at her tears. "Did you kill my mother's baby too? What kind of man are you?" She collapses on the stairs, head in her hands, and cries, hysterical, loud, noisy sobs at first, then more rhythmic gulps, until she's hiccupping and cold. Her father sits beside her, immobile, impassive, until she has finished.

"That's not the way it was," he says, finally.

"I remember," she says. "That day when you came home and found them. Don't lie to me. I'm not stupid."

And she's in the car and it's 1967, the motor's running and the snow has covered all the windows. She pretends it's a snow fort, but she has no toys to play with and she wants to go inside. Then she hears a loud explosion. Another. *Gunshots,* she thinks now. *Extinction.* She's four years old and although she tries to open the car door, it's too hard. She can't see out the windows and she's frightened. In a couple of moments, Daddy returns, gets in and reverses the car all the way up to the highway. She tells him she's scared and he pats her hand. "Daddy's here," he says. "Don't be scared."

"Where are we going?" she asks him.

"Daddy's going to take to you to Angie's to play."

"But I didn't get my dolly," she says. "I want my dolly to take to Angie's."

Daddy sighs. "Can you play without your doll just for today, Pumpkin?" he says. "Daddy has to go back to work. You be a good girl and I'll be back soon, you'll see." He goes inside first and speaks to Angie's parents. Then he takes her out of the car and hands her to Angie. They wave goodbye. His car is covered in snow.

"I did not kill your mother," Joe says now. "I *loved* her."

Kate pummels him with her fists, saying, "You lying bastard!" over and over and he doesn't defend himself, so her fists sink into him, and he absorbs all her rage.

"I came home early that day," he says, slowly, "because I'd received an anonymous call at work. Everyone knew about your mother and … that man. It didn't seem right that she would brazenly bring him into our home … with you there …."

"The Skaters' Waltz." Iris and Danny pretend-skate on the porch, scarves flying, mittens on, while Kate watches through window. Now and then they stop, pick up the bottle on the ground, open it and take a swig. Then they continue, laughing, pretend-falling so that they have to catch each other. "That wasn't the only time he came here," she says now. "You must have known that."

"Yes. Iris ... your mother ... swore she was going to end it. We used to fight horribly about it." He turns to Kate. "I would have let her go, if that's what she wanted. I never tried to keep her here."

Kate shakes her head. The air bristles with frost.

"They were arguing when I arrived. You must remember that. He wanted her to leave with him. She didn't want to go. When I opened the door, they were upstairs, shouting. I called out and Iris came down the stairs .... Danny ... he'd taken a gun out of my cabinet. Iris was terrified. She called to me to help, but I couldn't get there in time ...." His voice breaks and he's silent for a moment. "*He* shot her," he says. "Not me. I shot *him*. In self-defence."

Kate lets the words and their meaning float around in her head. They're both dead, she thinks. Nobody to challenge him.

"There's so much you don't know about your mother," he says.

"Whose fault is that?" she says, sharp, a blizzard of ice needles in her brain.

"You were a child. She'd been carrying on for a long time —"

"I know all about it," she says. "I know more than you think." The phone rings, but neither of them moves. They remain silent through its seven echoes. "I spoke to Miranda Magos. Her Goan friend." She waits, to give him a chance to reply, to explain, presses her fingers into her temples.

He sighs deeply.

"Did you put my half-brother up for adoption?" she asks. "I have a right to know. Or did you kill him, too?"

"I had nothing to do with that baby," he says. "I know nothing about it."

"Yes, you do."

He shakes his head. "You've already made up your mind. Believe what you want."

"You're right," Kate says. "And so far, I don't believe much of what you've told me. You're just saving your ass."

"Kate, I swear it's the truth."

But she doesn't know to what truth he is referring. What if he and Elaine planned it all? What if the two of them were seeing each other all along? What if Elaine stepped into her mother's shoes? And what about Rose? Surely she doesn't know. She can't. Did Angie know? What did he do, keep everyone away from the house while he packed and put away everything that belonged to Iris? What did he tell people, and wasn't he upset? Didn't *anyone* get suspicious? They'd watched Iris' parade of infidelities, cringed at her father's embarrassment. But did they believe she deserved to die? And if not, how could a woman vanish with no consequence? It seems extraordinary, she thinks, but of course, it isn't. Patti's disappearance would have gone unheeded had it not been for the discovery of her motorcycle. Joe was much too clever to leave anything like that behind. He was also the only police officer at that time. He could have disposed of anything. She presses her fingers into her temples. "Who else knows about this?"

"Nobody knows," he says, passionately, his hand grasping her arm. "You've got to believe that."

She shakes off his hand. "So far you've lied to me about everything that concerns my mother. For all I know, you and Elaine planned it." She imagines, for a moment, her mother as a human sacrifice, lying on a pedestal, dressed in white, surrounded by statuettes and carvings in gold, silver, wood and spondylus. The vision dissolves into her mother's face: she is no more a deity than those beautiful children. The Inca priests used a blow to the back of the head; he used a bullet.

"Elaine had *nothing* to do with this," he says vehemently. "*Nothing*. She only just found out. That's why she .... Blame me. Not Elaine. Do you understand?"

"No, I don't understand," Kate says. She pulls the quilt tight around her, buries her face in the scent. *Understanding is a thirteen-letter word. Perhaps the length of the word itself keeps us apart.* "If it happened the way you said, why didn't you turn yourself in?"

"I didn't go to the authorities because the two of them, both shot with my guns, in my house ... I didn't think I stood much of a chance. And what would have happened to you?" He puts his arm around her shoulder.

She stiffens.

"I wanted to protect you," he says. "*I* knew the truth. I made a choice I figured I could live with."

"What about me?" she says. "Did you ever wonder how I'd live with this?"

"I didn't think you'd ever find out," he says, misunderstanding.

She thinks about her flimsy relationships, her abandoning men, her fear of genuine emotions, her overwhelming distrust. She has made a life of extinguishing her feelings. "Can't you see that I would have lived a different life had I known my mother was dead? But to make me believe she discarded me ....What right did you have?" She turns to him, and they stare at each other, mute, engulfed by the devastating power unleashed between them.

He shakes his head, his eyes penitent, anguished. Squeezes her shoulder.

A burial fixes a point in time.

She gets up and walks down the steps. In her hands, the letters rustle, the ink old, indelible, her lifelong longing solidified between the lines of careful words. All that white space.

"Kate," her father calls.

She continues down the stairs, into the car, ignition, gears. *What is left out?*

"I didn't realize ... Kate!" he calls, his voice desperate.

She inches forward, and now he is the one huddled on the top step, waiting. In the dark, she can only see his silhouette — a dark shape. *Daddy, Dad, Father.* And it's not the ending to any fairy tale she knows.

"I'm sorry," he says, the shape says. "Kate, please ...."

But it's not enough. It can never be enough.

At the highway, she stops, unsure which way to turn. *Home.* Direction? Bearing? She shakes her head. Night fills her eyes. *I'm sorry*, her father says in her head. *Nineteen years and he didn't even embrace me.*

She swings onto the highway, propelled by the spectre of memory, tracing Iris, windows down, the cool night air tearing her eyes. Parks the car on the shoulder and walks into the dark, stumbles up and down rows of stumps — crosses, signposts. *Lost and found. Mingled dust.* For a moment, she imagines Iris swimming through sand and soil, surfacing to confirm or deny Joe's story. Bones floating to the surface. The past two weeks fast-forward through her brain as if they were clouds changing shape at hurtling speed, or flowers blossoming in seconds, or mountains rising and sinking in one breath.

The letters catch immediately. Her words explode into fans of fire. She cups her hands to hold them, even when they burn her palms, cups her hands to contain the withering edges, which shrink farther and farther into ash. When they are spent, she rubs her hands together, and blows.

ACKNOWLEDGEMENTS

Many thanks to Frank Hook, Brian Burke, Verbena Donati-Jenkins, Carolyn Smart and Diane Watson for reading early drafts of this novel and offering their insightful comments and encouragement.

I would like to thank the many people in Twisp who took the time to speak to me, especially Vern and Beulah La Motte, who welcomed me into their home and recounted their early memories of the Methow Valley.

Special thanks to Joy Gugeler for being able to see my vision, for her valuable editing and for her enthusiastic response. Thanks, too, to my agent, Carolyn Swayze, for her continued support, and to the Canada Council for its generous assistance during the writing of this novel.

OTHER RAINCOAST FICTION:

Sounding the Blood by Amanda Hale
1-55192-484-6 $21.95 CDN $15.95 US

Small Accidents by Andrew Gray
1-55192-508-7 $19.95 CDN $14.95 US

Quicksilver by Nadine McInnis
1-55192-482-x $19.95 CDN $14.95 US

Write Turns: New Directions in Canadian Fiction
1-55192-402-1 $24.95 CDN $19.95 US

Slow Lightning by Mark Frutkin
1-55192-406-4 $21.95 CDN $16.95 US

After Battersea Park by Jonathan Bennett
1-55192-408-0 $21.95 CDN $16.95 US

Kingdom of Monkeys by Adam Lewis Schroeder
1-55192-404-8 $19.95 CDN $14.95 US

Finnie Walsh by Steven Galloway
1-55192-372-6 $21.95 CDN $16.95 US

Hotel Paradiso by Gregor Robinson
1-55192-358-0 $21.95 CDN $16.95 US

Rhymes with Useless by Terence Young
1-55192-354-8 $18.95 CDN $14.95 US

Song of Ascent by Gabriella Goliger
1-55192-374-2 $18.95 CDN $14.95 US